ALISTAIR IN WONDERLAND

A WONDERLAND EVER AFTER NOVEL

ARIELLA ZOELLE

Cover Design by Natasha of Natasha Snow Designs

Editing by Pam of Undivided Editing

Proofreading by Sandra of One Love Editing

ISBN: 978-1-954202-15-3

DEDICATION

This is for everyone who has ever wanted to follow the White Rabbit to Wonderland to have a fun adventure of their own.

T he only thing I liked about hobnobbing was that it sounded like a euphemism for a blow job. It was pretty ironic, considering being forced to hobnob for work really sucked.

As I sulked in the beautiful ballroom packed full of rich donors to fleece for my shitty job, I couldn't help but wish one of the hot guys from catering would "hobnob" my dick instead. See? It sounds so dirty!

Of course, I was all talk. Nobody had hobnobbed or sucked my dick before, and the only thing that had ever fucked me was life—and it didn't even have the decency to use any lube.

As I tried not to despair over the garbage hand dealt to me compliments of the cosmic universe, I stared up at the ornate mural on the ceiling of gods frolicking in the clouds. What was up with rich people painting flying babies with their dicks out and having the audacity to call it art? I wondered how wealthy you needed to be before that creepy impulse for having cherubs with chubbies got recategorized as being classy?

"It's understandable that you're having an emotional crisis over the vases here being worth more than your life, but could you at least *try* to act like you aren't?" Harriet von Frobisher chided, sounding every bit as pretentious as her stupid name. Ugh, my boss was the absolute *worst*. "Or is this a pathetic strategy to get the donors to pity you enough to take out their checkbooks?"

Questions like that were the reason I regularly fantasized about baking a "Fuck this shit, I quit" cake. A caterer walked by with a tray of canapés, so I grabbed one and held it up to my boss. "I'll get back to bilking these billionaires out of their fortunes right after I finish this," I said in a cheery voice to hide how much I hated everything to do with my god-awful work.

"Either start getting donations, or you can find yourself a new job." She gave a disdainful sniff before sauntering off to go schmooze some old guy out of the money that would have gone to his fourth wife in a few years.

I was about to eat the appetizer I had grabbed until I saw it looked like a rabbit shit on some salmon that was stacked on a five-day-old stale crouton garnished with grass. "Oh, *yuck*." There was no way in hell I would put that in my mouth.

Desperate to dump it, I considered being spiteful enough to toss it into one of those ugly vases that my boss believed were worth more than my pathetic excuse for a life. But I knew it would be some poor bastard like me who would be stuck cleaning it up and getting in trouble for the rotting smell, so I couldn't do that to them. Instead, I ditched it at a nearby table before I did my best to disappear on the fringe of the large party.

The sudden feeling of a man pressing close against my back made me stiffen in surprise. His deep voice had my dick's immediate attention as he murmured in my ear, "You look like you want to run away." His sexy British accent got me all hot and bothered, which outweighed my outrage at being manhandled by some entitled billionaire looking for a new boy toy.

His cologne was a dark, woodsy scent that stirred desire within me. The romantic in me wanted to breathe him in deep and give myself over to whatever sinful pleasures he wished to bestow upon me. The horny-virgin part of my brain was ready for him to bend me over the nearest table and fuck me in front of everyone until I screamed his name while I came harder than I ever had in my life. I had never experienced such a visceral reaction to a person before. It was a little disorienting.

When I didn't react, he reached out and wrapped an

arm around my waist. He pulled me flush against his firm body as his lips ghosted over the tip of my ear in a way that made me go weak in the knees as my cock grew rock hard.

My gaze darted around the room to make sure everyone was ignoring us. Somehow, the world had gone into slow motion, as if I was a step outside of time, with the man pressed against my back. Satisfied that no one was paying attention, I finally found my voice. "Can you blame me?"

His dark chuckle reverberated through me, filling me with a lustful need to ride his cock until I came all over his stomach. "Not at all. It's so dreadfully dull here." I stiffened with a startled noise when he traced the shell of my ear with his tongue, putting me at risk of coming in my pants like a teenager with no self-control. "Shall we entertain ourselves with an adventure somewhere a little more private?"

My cock was desperately interested in what was being offered. I had never done more than kiss a guy before, but if the man was even half as hot as his voice sounded, I'd be down to let him do anything he wanted to me. Hell, if he was only a tenth as sexy as the fantasy version of him in my head, he could buy me with his millions for his personal collection. Screw having morals. At least I'd *finally* have sex.

Curious about the handsome stranger, I turned to face him. I had been prepared to see a gross ogre of a skeezy rich guy ogling me, but he was the most beautiful man I had ever seen in my life. He appeared to have been born from moonlight, stardust, and dreams come true. Dressed in a white suit with a metallic pink vest and tie, he resembled a prince who had stepped out of the pages of a fairy tale. His hair, eyebrows, and eyelashes were pure white, giving him a striking appearance. He had the most unusual dark pink eyes, which were bright with amusement at my stunned expression. Although they were probably contacts, they looked startlingly real.

The combined effect of his appearance and scent sparked my arousal into a roaring blaze. I didn't disguise the fact that I was fully erect because when someone was that sexy, he was probably used to it. I swallowed hard as I gazed up at him in awe. "What kind of adventure?"

"One that is worthy of someone as remarkable as you."

I wanted to laugh at the absurdity that there was anything remarkable about me, but there was genuine admiration in his expression that stopped me. "Who are you?"

"Someone who has been waiting a *very* long time to meet you." There should have been a law that somebody that attractive wasn't allowed to say something so swoony to a hopeless-romantic virgin like me.

"Meet *me*?" That didn't make sense.

His smile was so dazzling I almost needed to grab onto him to steady myself. "Indeed. I'm looking forward to getting better acquainted with you." He held his hand out to me. "Come with me."

For some strange reason, something deep inside me was ready to follow him to the end of the Earth, if that's where he wanted to go. While I was probably being overly naïve, and it would come back to haunt me, I figured that being dead in a dumpster had to be better than being stuck in my shitastic job and meaningless life. At least if I went out with a bang, I'd have no regrets.

When I was a kid, my favorite book had been *Alice in Wonderland*. I had always dreamed of visiting that world, and now the sexy human equivalent to the White Rabbit was standing right in front of me. Why shouldn't I follow the gorgeous albino prince down the rabbit hole and see where I landed?

Without a single moment of hesitation, I put my hand in his and followed him for what I hoped would be the start of a sensual adventure.

After almost two centuries of searching, I had *finally* found my Alice. And he was even more beautiful and amazing than I had dared to hope. His powerful magic was constrained under its seals, begging me to release it from the bonds that had trapped it for so long. But it would have to wait until I had brought him to Wonderland.

I led him into a distant library down several hallways, which had a prominent silver filigree mirror as its focal point. It pulsed with ancient power as it commanded me to take Alice back to the Kingdom of Hearts without delay. I fully intended to, but my beast made things difficult by rattling against its cage, clamoring to make Alice's magic ours. It was a startling urge when my beast normally lay dormant. Not once in my long life had I ever experienced the need to claim anyone.

I owed it to my king and country to set aside my desires, but that small taste I had of Alice in the ball-room left me hungry for more. Not to mention the scent of his prominent arousal was driving me wild with lust.

With his fair blond hair, wide blue eyes, and well-tailored suit, he was as beautiful as the prophecy had promised. I took deliberate steps toward him, backing him up until he bumped against a bookcase. I pinned him in place with an arm over his shoulder on the shelf behind him, allowing his hard length to press against me. My hand trembled as I caressed his soft cheek. "I've waited such a long time to find you, Alice."

His eyebrows wrinkled with annoyance. "It's Alistair Hargreaves."

So that was his name now. "How fitting." I'd have to be careful not to call him Alice in the future. Thankfully, after spending so many years searching for him, he didn't disappoint. Although Alice wasn't mine, his intoxicating arousal called to my white rabbit heritage and begged me to satisfy him. I stroked his delicate cheekbone with my thumb. "You're even more beautiful than I had dared dream."

"Who are you?"

I was the private secretary and chief mage to the King of Hearts. The important task of finding Wonderland's long-lost Alice had been entrusted to me. But those were details that would have to wait for later. "You may call me Bianco."

When he wetted his lips while looking up at me with desire in his blue eyes, it broke my self-restraint. With his arousal clouding my senses, I caved to my beast's instincts as I promised myself it would only be one kiss. I leaned down and brushed my lips against his. The magic of Alice sparked under its restraining bonds when he kissed me back with passion. He was so soft and pliant under me as he let my tongue tease him into a frenzied need. The scrape of his nails against my scalp as he ran his fingers through my long hair was almost enough to unleash my beast.

My good intentions to only give him one kiss were put in peril when he rocked his erection against mine. Everything inside me begged to satisfy his needs, to care for Alice the way he deserved, and unify our magic by binding him to me forever. If I didn't regain control, I would take things too far. As much as I didn't want to, I forced distance between us.

He looked up at me with blue eyes darkened with lust. "Why did you stop?"

I traced his lower lip with my thumb as I fought my instincts to lay claim to him and his magic. "Because I won't be able to make myself stop if we continue any further."

He ran his hands up my chest to rest on my shoulders, looking up at me through lowered lashes. "What if I want you to keep going?"

It was almost impossible to resist him. My sense of duty warred with my desires. But Alistair's pheromones clouded my senses, making it a serious challenge to do what I must. I trailed my nose along the curve of his neck as I breathed him in deep, letting my tongue dart out to taste his sweetness. It filled my veins with fire as my beast begged me to take what was so willingly being offered. My voice came out in a dark rumble. "You are far too tempting to ask such questions."

"Please, Bianco." He took my hand and cupped it around his hardness. "I don't want to go back out there like this. And didn't you promise me an adventure?"

His plea shattered my weak resistance. I fell to my knees in front of him as I unfastened his pants to gain access. He wasn't mine to mate, but it *was* part of my royal responsibilities to take care of *all* of Alice's needs. And he had a mighty need, indeed. I lowered his trousers and briefs to reveal the ultimate temptation.

I leaned forward to tease his erection with my tongue before guiding him into my mouth. He sagged against the bookcase with a soft whimper as I bobbed along his length. His magic crackled under the restraints containing his power, begging me to bind him to me for the rest of time. But that was a pleasure I would never be allowed to have.

His hand found purchase in my hair. He gasped as

he gave me a gentle caress. "Wow, your hair is *so* soft. It's almost like bunny fur."

I huffed in amusement around his length in my mouth at how close he unintentionally came to guessing my heritage. The beast within me struggled to come to the surface to claim Alistair as ours by binding his magic to ours. But I shoved him down as I focused on pleasuring the savior of Wonderland. I was already taking enough liberties with my professional role as it was to enjoy such an intimate moment. But it was hard to regret it when the scent of our lusty pheromones mixing made me almost drunk as I sucked his prick with the greatest of pleasures.

He bit his lower lip to smother a whimper as he pushed deeper into my mouth. I took him to the base as I let my throat work him. When I moaned around him, he came with a soft cry. The taste of him on my tongue made my beast stir in its cage, demanding I take things to the next level and claim Alistair and his magic for ours. But I resisted my instincts as I leaned back on my haunches and looked up at him with smug satisfaction that I had taken such good care of him.

"*Wow.*" He stared at me with amazement as I helped him redress. "Wait, your eyes..."

When my beast surged forward, they took on an unnatural glow. I blinked as I settled myself, allowing them to return to normal. "We should get going."

"But what about you?" He looked at the visible tent in my pants.

I checked my gold pocket watch. We definitely didn't have time for me to give in to any more of my urges. I had already done too much as it was. Besides, it was my royal duty to take care of Alice, not the other way around. "It'll have to wait. We're late enough as it is."

He tilted his head as he regarded me while buttoning his pants. "Late for what?"

"For our fun adventure." Although it was difficult to leave his side, I walked over to the enormous mirror. I adjusted myself as best I could while chastising my unruly beast, who was raging inside about stopping so suddenly when we burned for Alice.

"What are you talking about?"

I gave him an enigmatic smile and a flirty wink over my shoulder. "Follow me and find out." With those words, I stepped into the mirror to return to Wonderland. Would Alistair be as brave as his ancestor to take his rightful place as the new Alice of the Kingdom of Hearts?

CHAPTER
THREE
ALISTAIR

I stared in shock at the place where Bianco had been standing a moment ago before I watched him disappear. It was such a strange occurrence that it was enough to distract me from the glee that I had enjoyed the first blow job of my life. Was I hallucinating, or had that really happened?

Hurrying over to the mirror, I hesitantly brought my hand up to the glass. It rippled under my touch like water, with the waves getting bigger as my fingers slid through it into cold nothingness. "What the hell?" I watched in amazement as my entire hand, wrist, and then my forearm slipped through the same way Bianco had disappeared.

The smart thing would have been to pull back, pretend nothing ever happened, and go back to work. But I hated my shitastic job and my asshole coworkers and had nothing waiting for me at home except for boring chores. I didn't even have plants! Talk about pathetic.

There was nothing stopping me from living my own *Alice in Wonderland* type of adventure. I wrapped my courage around me and stepped through the mirror before I could think better of it.

It startled me when I plunged headfirst into the darkness. I yelped as I plummeted so far that down became up as the world was turned on its side. The echo seemed to stretch forever in both directions. It was terrifying as I tumbled into the nothingness surrounding me.

I fell for so long that my fear faded away as I grew impatient to land. Finally, I saw a glimmer of light above me that became below me as I continued my endless descent into the unknown. As a black-and-white checkerboard floor came into view, I braced for the bone-shattering impact that was sure to hurt like hell if it didn't outright kill me. But a gust of wind caught me, allowing me to drift down to stand without so much as a wince.

Straightening my red suit jacket as I looked around, I was alone in a grand hall that seemed to stretch out in both directions for an eternity, with an endless row of doors on either side of me. The room was lit with flickering candles that gave it an eerie atmosphere that I didn't like at all.

There was no trace of the man I had followed through the mirror. I tentatively called out, "Bianco?" When there was no answer, I repeated his name louder. The echo of it bounced off the walls in search of him, but I was very much alone in an unknown place.

My only company was the sound of flickering candles and an ominous clock ticking somewhere unseen. There was a table in the middle of the room that had a gold skeleton key on it and a glass bottle with a sparkling purple liquid inside. Around the bottleneck was a white label with ornate golden calligraphy that said, "Drink Me."

Wait, had I seriously fallen down a rabbit hole into the world of *Alice in Wonderland*? But that was impossible...wasn't it? For one, it would mean I got the best blow job ever from the *real* White Rabbit. Secondly, it would mean I was a part of my favorite childhood book. It just wasn't possible.

But what if I had? What if I really was lucky enough to leave behind my meaningless life in the real world to come to Wonderland? Bianco *had* called me Alice. And before Mom died when I was a kid, she had always talked about us being descendants of the real Alice Liddell, even though I never believed her. But what if I was Alice reborn?

No, those were absurd thoughts. Despite that, the feeling that I had landed in Wonderland wouldn't leave me. Standing around waiting for Bianco wouldn't get me anywhere fast, so I embraced the spirit of whimsy of the books and retraced Alice's steps.

I first tested the key in the tiny door that looked like a fancy entrance to a mousehole. To my delight, it swung open without effort. I got down on my hands and knees to peer through it, amazed to see the spectacular forest described in the book. I left the door open and pocketed the key before I braved drinking some of the glittering potion that tasted like sparkling blueberry wine.

It suffused me with warmth as the world became quite large. When I was the perfect size to go through the miniature door, I realized my gamble had paid off. I sealed the bottle before slipping it into my pocket.

Off to the side was a tiny table with cute petit fours. On top of the stacked blue-and-white china tray, there was a decorative label with gold glitter calligraphy that said, "Eat Me." I picked a white one with a heart-shaped red rose and walked through the door. Everything outside was huge and green, with sunlight filtering through the leaves of the trees as a refreshing breeze brushed by me. There were all kinds of foreign bird-songs and animal sounds I had never heard before.

As cool as it was to experience, it made me fearful that some strange creature might come along and mistake me for food. I took the tiniest nibble of the cake to grow. Instead of shooting up to the tops of the giant woods surrounding me, I grew back to my regular size.

However, since it was a golden opportunity, I took another bite of the Eat Me cake to add a few extra inches to my height, because why the fuck not? Maybe if I got lucky, my dick would grow in proportion, too. Satisfied with my new stature, I pocketed the rest of the cake in case I needed it later.

Looking around the area, I still didn't see any trace of the man who had brought me to the strange world. "Bianco?"

Silence was my only answer, so it was time to explore. I walked straight forward since it would be easier to backtrack without getting lost. As I made my way through the wild woods, I noticed strong incense wafting on the wind that gave me the hope I might come across somebody who could help me. If I really was living out the Wonderland books, that had to be a sign that I was nearing the famous Caterpillar.

When I entered a clearing, vibrant mushrooms grew higher than a human was tall. The toadstools seemed to change colors every time I blinked.

I shielded my eyes as I looked up to see if I could spy the notorious character from the books. Sure enough, on top of a huge red-and-purple mushroom with glittering spots, a beautiful man leaned back against a neighboring toadstool.

He smoked from a mirrored glass hookah, which was sitting on a shorter pink mushroom. His navy suit had sleeves trimmed in gold filigree that shimmered in the sunlight. He had rainbow-colored hair that cascaded around his face like a beautiful waterfall. His legs were impossibly long as he stretched them out on top of the mushrooms.

Everything about him exuded an air of elegance as he exhaled a puff of pale blue smoke in the shape of a caterpillar that morphed into a butterfly that flew down to me. When I held out my hand, it landed in my palm, flapping its smoky wings as it preened, before disappearing with a gusting breeze. Holy shit, was I actually meeting the famed Caterpillar from Alice's adventures?

Since everyone had been brimming full of British good manners in the novels, I figured it couldn't hurt to be super polite. I called out to him, "Excuse me, sir, but I was wondering if I could trouble you to tell me where I am?"

The man took a drag off the silver hookah pipe, holding it inside for a long moment before expelling the light blue puff of smoke. He pinned me under his gaze. Even at such a distance, his indigo eyes captivated me.

"You are here," he answered in a mellifluous tenor voice that sounded like music.

He may have been sexy, but it was still annoying that he had given such an unhelpful response. "Where is here?"

"Where you are."

I bristled at him acting as if that was the dumbest

question anyone had ever asked him. "And does 'here' have a name?"

He inhaled from the hookah pipe once more, waiting to reply until he exhaled. "The name of this place has no meaning for a stranger."

Like Alice, I had a low tolerance for bullshit, so his behavior was extra annoying. "I'd still like to know."

When he remained silent, I almost thought he wouldn't answer me. But after another puff, he deigned to reply. "This is the King of Hearts' forest."

I *was* about to celebrate my good fortune at being in Wonderland, but something was off. He had said it was a king and not a queen who was the ruler. Something wasn't adding up, so I tried to get confirmation. "Who are you?"

"I am me."

My indignation flared as he acted like that vague answer somehow explained everything. "*Really*?"

He became miffed at my sarcastic response. "Who else would I be if not me?"

Pinching the bridge of my nose while I drew a calming breath, I attempted a more direct tactic. "Do you have a name?"

"I do."

There was little consolation in knowing Alice had put up with the same vague nonsense answers in the past. Maybe that was why almost no one had names in Lewis Carroll's books. She must have given up because it was too much effort to get a name out of someone who talked in circles. "Will you please tell me?"

"Why do you wish to know?"

I huffed in annoyance. "Because not knowing is rude."

He looked unimpressed by my response. His indigo gaze assessed me, almost as if he were trying to decide if I was worthy of a response. "Who are you?"

Part of me wanted to throw his answer back in his face, but it wouldn't help. For once in my life, I decided not to be petty. "I'm Alistair Hargreaves. Bianco brought me here, but we were separated. Have you seen him?"

The stranger dressed all in blue put down the hookah pipe and stood up. To my shock, the person I had thought was the famous Caterpillar sprouted rainbow butterfly wings and gracefully flew down to stand in front of me. Every flap was like colorful jewels sparkling in the sunlight.

Despite my newly acquired extra inches, he towered over me. If everyone in Wonderland was as tall as him, I was definitely going to eat more growing cake later.

Whatever he had smoked had a floral, fruity smell that made me dizzy and a bit tingly all over. Was it possible to get a contact high?

That close, I could see there were gold flecks in his uncanny eyes. I got lost looking into their depths, which seemed to stare right through me. It was almost as if he was hypnotizing me.

He hummed with interest. "So, you are Alice?"

"Alistair."

There was an approval in his gaze that made me feel good. He didn't seem to be the easily impressed type. "Bianco chose well."

I couldn't even pretend to understand what he meant by that cryptic comment. "What do you mean?"

"Despite your incessant questioning, you are quite appealing."

Why did hearing that make me happy? I should have been furious at his treatment of me, but being so close to him made me feel almost high. "Will you please tell me your name?"

"I am Vivalter."

It was a relief to finally find out his name. I expected him to keep bullshitting me like in the books. "How do you know Bianco?"

"There is no one in Wonderland who does not know Bianco."

It was like being back in free fall in the darkness as he confirmed I had somehow done the impossible and ended up in the world of my favorite book. How was that possible when it was a work of fiction made up in the 1860s? If he was right, then I had actually gotten an awesome blow job from the White Rabbit. *What in the actual entire fuck?*

I pushed aside my confusion to get more concrete

answers from the evasive man. "Why does everyone know Bianco? Is he famous?"

"As the private secretary and chief mage to the king, Bianco is indeed quite famous. Where have you come from where you are unaware of his status?"

"New York."

Vivalter shrugged with a dismissive wave of his hand. "Never heard of it. Places in the realms beyond Wonderland are useless to me."

Rather than continuing down that fascinating path, I refocused my attention. "Could you please help me find Bianco? I need to get back to him."

"You are where you should be."

He said it with too much confidence for my comfort. "I mean, I'm technically supposed to be at a fundraiser event in New York, not in the middle of some strange forest. Wonderland is just a—" I stopped myself from saying it was only a made-up book. Telling someone he was fictional was a pretty asshole move. "It's the stuff of legends where I come from."

"What matters is not from whence you came. It only matters where you're going," Vivalter said. "You belong to us, Alice."

The longer I looked up into Vivalter's eyes and breathed in his intoxicating scent, the more confused I became. It made it too hard to think, which was an enormous fucking problem when I was in a place where I didn't know what to think to begin with.

I jumped at the sound of someone clearing their throat behind me. To my great relief, it was Bianco. Without thinking, I threw my arms around him as I hugged him tight. "Oh, I'm *so* glad you found me!" And I wasn't just saying that because I was hoping for another blow job, and I didn't want to walk miles through a forest alone in search of him.

When he embraced me, it felt like coming home, as if I had finally found the place where I belonged. It didn't make any sense when I lived by myself in a world that didn't want me, and we had just met. But something inside of me reached out to Bianco, begging him to stay with me forever. Deep down in my heart of hearts, I somehow trusted that as long as he was by my side, I would be okay. I wasn't sure where that certainty came from, but I didn't care. Fuck it, I was in Wonderland! It was the one place where logic wasn't required, right?

"You certainly wasted no time in taking proper care of Alice," Vivalter said in a tone of voice that implied he somehow knew about our sexy adventure in the library.

"It is my job to tend to *all* of his needs," Bianco said, making my dick stir with interest once more at the innuendo. I sure hoped that was code for fuck me stupid later. "If you'll excuse us, we are needed elsewhere."

"Very well. I shall bid you farewell for now, but we will have words later, Bianco." There was something ominous about his parting, but it was amazing watching him fly away with his beautiful rainbow wings.

After the dizzying effects of Vivalter's incense, it was a terrible idea to be so close to Bianco, who smelled so good it made my dick hard again. I took a step back and shook my head to clear it. "Okay, before we go anywhere, I have some questions, starting with why do the two of you keep calling me Alice instead of Alistair?"

Bianco gestured for me to follow him. "Because you are our new Alice."

"But that doesn't make any sense! In case you missed it, I'm not a girl," I protested.

His lips turned up in a smirk that made my heart tumble down eighty-seven flights of stairs and into a wall as I remembered them wrapped around my cock earlier. "Believe me, I'm *very* aware of your maleness."

My cheeks flushed bright red despite myself. "Are you seriously the White Rabbit from *Alice in Wonderland*?"

"Indeed I am."

Did getting a blow job from a fictional character in a children's book mean I was going to Hell? It seemed like the kind of thing that would earn me a one-way ticket in a handbasket to go high-five the devil for committing such an awesome sin before I burned in eternal damnation. I stated the obvious, simply because my mind was still boggling too much to do anything else. "Also, news flash: I'm American! How can I be Alice if I'm not British?"

"You are a descendant of the original Alice, which is why you are our new Alice, despite your nationality being different."

The information amazed me. "Wow, I guess my mom was right about us being related after all." I let myself be wowed for a moment before I refocused my attention. "So, what's the significance of me being your new Alice?"

"You are the key to saving Wonderland."

I blanched at the revelation. "That sure as shit sounds like I'm about to risk my life as the savior in a holy crusade war against Wonderland's enemies."

He glanced over at me with amusement. "What a vivid imagination you have."

"Oh, you don't even know the half of it, buddy." It made me feel good when he laughed. "And that wasn't a 'no,' so you better hurry up and get to the part where you lay my fears to rest before I panic."

"There are no wars, no enemies, no dangers awaiting you anywhere in Wonderland," Bianco said in a soothing voice. "You are not in any danger. And I would certainly protect you with my life if it ever arose."

It was hard not to be distracted by the mental picture of me clinging to Bianco, who wore a suit of armor in my fantasy and held me with one arm and a sword in his other hand while wind ruffled his hair like we were the cover photo on a romance novel. Damn it, I was too much of a hopeless romantic for him to say swoony stuff like that to me.

Clearing my throat, I tried to make myself focus. "Okay, so if I'm not in danger, then why am I here?"

"Because I promised you a fun adventure," Bianco said with a wink that almost made me stumble. "I will explain everything on the way to the palace. Will you come with me?"

The chickenshit part of me wanted to run away from any hint of responsibility. But when I had nothing keeping me in the real world, why shouldn't I embrace the cosmic universe doing me a solid by giving me a redo where I was allowed to live a life that actually mattered and had fun while doing it?

In the end, the decision was the easiest one I had ever made. "You know what? Fuck, yeah! Let's go on an awesome adventure. Maybe we can have some sexy shenanigans on the way."

T here was something incredibly charming about Alistair's enthusiastic embrace of his new role. I had been prepared for him to beg me to take him home, but he seemed relieved that he didn't need to return to his world. It made me even more excited to go on an adventure with him to bring the magic back to Wonderland.

"So, if you're the White Rabbit, does that make Vivalter the Caterpillar from *Alice in Wonderland*?" Alistair asked as we began the walk to the palace. "Because I thought he was until he sprouted wings."

"Yes, Vivalter is the Caterpillar you know from the books, but he transcended into being the Butterfly quite some time ago."

Alistair glanced over at me with curiosity. "Does

that mean you both have animal forms? Or was that just part of the story Lewis Carroll made up?"

"We are indeed shifters who can take on a human or animal form. When I first approached Alice, since she was a young girl, it would have been improper to do so in this form. Being a smaller rabbit intrigued her imagination more, leading her to follow me to Wonderland."

The possibility seemed to excite him. "You can really turn into a rabbit?"

"If the occasion calls for it, I can be as small as a house pet or as large as a Jabberwocky. However, I much prefer my current state. It makes it easier to do the things I need to do."

He bit his lower lip as he debated asking his next question. "Is it wildly inappropriate to ask if you could show me?"

"I will happily do so once we are back at the palace."

He glanced over at me. "I'm curious. Why did you originally seek out Alice?"

"Because the prophecies said she was the one who would save Wonderland from the great darkness. You are clearly familiar with the books, but there is a great deal more to the story than what was written." When he didn't comment, I continued. "Alice returned in her teenage years to stop the war between the kingdoms. She saved many lives with her actions, but there were unexpected consequences that continue to put Wonderland in peril to this day."

"What happened?"

"When all was resolved, Alice returned to Over-land," I explained. "What none of us anticipated was that she took her magic with her, leaving Wonderland to die a very slow death."

His brow wrinkled in confusion. "Why would she do that after fighting so hard to save it?"

"It was not something she did intentionally. Indeed, she would have been quite distraught if she knew what had happened after she returned home for the last time. It was a disastrous mistake made by my predecessor that we have lived with for almost two centuries."

"What was the mistake?"

I sighed with old frustrations. "Oscuro was the Black Rabbit and personal mage of the former Queen of Hearts. Since the kingdoms had been using dark magic to commit such violent aggressions against each other, he thought it best to seal it inside of Alice for safe-keeping to take with her when she left for the final time. But he didn't just seal the dark magic that had caused the problems during the war. He accidentally locked away most of the light magic, too. So when Alice returned home and was unable to return, Wonderland lost almost all of its magic."

Alistair puzzled his way through the issue. "But Vivalter said you were the king's mage, which means you must be able to use magic, right?"

"Indeed. Anyone who had close contact with the

original Alice was largely unaffected by Oscuro's mistake. That is why there are very few of us left who have magical powers. It's why I had to come find you."

A hint of fear appeared in his eyes. "So, you're saying all that dark and light magic is contained within me?"

"Yes, it is locked away inside you with the spells Oscuro placed on the original Alice. My intention is to release the light magic so that Wonderland may thrive once more. The kingdom is dying a slow death without it. That is why there are no flowers left that can sing their beautiful songs and the card guards disappeared long ago. Without magic to sustain them, they cannot exist."

He held his hand over his heart. "But what about the dark magic? Won't it also be released and cause wars to happen again?"

"No, because I will purify it so that no harm will ever befall Wonderland again." I reached over and took his hand in mine to give it a reassuring squeeze. "You have my word that it won't hurt you. With all due respect to my predecessor, I am a much stronger mage than him. I have also studied the prophecies to learn what I must do."

"What prophecies?"

As the royal seer, Vivalter had given the Hearts royal family countless prophecies with unfailing accuracy. The ones regarding Alice were words I had studied extensively over my centuries of service to the crown. "They say that when a descendant of Alice returns, a bonding love will form in their heart to unlock the magic to restore Wonderland to the majesty it once was."

Alistair pulled his hand from mine. "Wait, are you telling me I have to fall in love with someone?"

His reaction puzzled me. "I believe it is referring to a bond of love you will form with Wonderland that will enable you to save it. There is no mention of a person."

He sighed with relief. "Then everything might be okay."

It was a strange reaction. "Why do you say that?"

"Because I've loved Wonderland since I read the books as a kid. I can't get another person to love me to save my life."

The mention of Alistair with another love made my beast rattle in its cage again. It couldn't bear the thought of someone who wasn't us touching him and bringing him pleasure. "Perhaps it's because you haven't met the right person yet." *Or perhaps it's because you hadn't met us yet*, my beast whispered in the shadows of my heart.

He hesitated for a moment. "Do you have a partner?"

"No, my life is dedicated to serving the King of Hearts."

He seemed intrigued by my answer. "Are you in love with him?"

I arched an eyebrow at his forwardness. "That's quite a presumptuous question."

His cheeks flushed a becoming shade of pink as his expression became sheepish. "Sorry. You're right, that was an asshole assumption. My bad."

"While I have been friends with King Rei since he was a child, the love we share is brotherly. He is also far too dedicated to his kingdom to allow himself the privilege of openly loving someone."

My response appeared to surprise him. "Wait, you're telling me the King of Hearts isn't in love?"

"That is a complication best left unsaid."

"Why?"

Before I could say anything further, there was a suspicious rustling in the trees. I held in a sigh at the predictability of a most unpredictable creature as I stopped Alistair from continuing forward. "Because if you speak of the devil, he almost always appears."

CHAPTER
FIVE
ALISTAIR

Before I could ask what Bianco meant, the rustling in the trees above revealed a thick, fluffy tail with ombre fur the color of a magnificent sunset. The vibrant purple, pink, and orange pattern spread until a giant cat appeared. It lacked the traditional stripes I had always associated with him, but he had a most unmistakable grin and glowing amber eyes.

"When I am a Dëvîlskātž, what better devil to appear than the best of cats?" His tail swished as he snickered to himself at his own joke. "If you wish to speak of our great king, I am all ears." He faded away until only his ears remained, which flicked at the sound of distant birdsong.

My awe made it impossible to stay silent. "Holy shit! You're Cheshire!" Along with the White Rabbit, the quirky cat was one of my favorite characters from Lewis Carroll's books.

"Indeed I am." He returned to full form as he dangled an arm off the tree branch and looked down at me with intrigue. "And you are an even more curious creature than a cat. Who might you be?"

"I'm Alistair. It's so nice to meet you!" I did my best not to fanboy too much. The last thing I wanted to do was embarrass myself in front of my favorite characters from the books.

Cheshire jumped down from the tree and walked over to rub against my legs to beg for attention. "Alistair, you say? You don't *smell* like an Alistair."

It was hard to resist the urge to reach down and scritch behind his ears when I adored cats. But it seemed pretty improper when he could talk. "I'm Alistair Hargreaves."

"Funny, you smell like an Alice." It startled me when Cheshire suddenly shifted into a tall man right in front of my eyes. However, his furry cat ears and tail remained. He wore a dapper, dark violet three-piece suit that made his sunset ombre hair that fell around his face in gentle waves more stunning. But his glowing amber eyes were spellbinding as he grinned down at me in a charming manner. "You also smell like my brother. How unfair you met him first."

I blinked in shock. "Vivalter is your *brother*?" That

seemed like an important detail that was left out of the original books.

His tail swished behind him with amusement. "In ancient times, caterpillars were known as the devil's cats. Thus, he is a Dëvîlskātž, the same as me. After all, he was a *cat*erpillar once. It is only natural that he is the brother of a grand Cheshire cat such as myself."

Now that I knew they were related, I could see the familial resemblance in their handsome faces and fabulous hair. "That's amazing!"

He shocked me when he leaned down and nuzzled against my neck with a moan that sent a shiver through me. "Oh, how we have missed our playful Alice! Think of all the fun we can have together now that you're no longer a young girl with prim-and-proper manners."

It surprised me when Bianco tugged me back from the affectionate Cheshire. "You can have plenty of fun without Alistair."

Cheshire morphed into his large cat form, headbutting Bianco in the shins. "But our king refuses to play with me," he said with a dramatic sigh. He reached up and kneaded at his jacket before Bianco brushed his paws away. "Can't you put in a good word for the ol' Cheshire cat? I'm so lonely without my favorite toy."

"Perhaps if you treated King Rei less like a toy, he might not be as resistant to your overtures."

"That man is so stubborn; I swear he's part cat." His annoyance morphed into a very Cheshire grin. "I suppose he acts that way to make it more fun for me to chase him."

"I don't think that's why he rejects your advances," Bianco said with a hint of a smirk. "It's a great deal more complicated than that."

Cheshire turned into the size of a kitten and jumped up to sit on my shoulder. "Then it is a good thing I am the most stubborn of stubborn cats. Very well. I shall accompany you to the palace."

"Have you forgotten that you're still banned from your last stunt?" Amusement colored Bianco's tone.

It made me curious. "What happened?"

"I might have given an effective demonstration to show King Rei that, unlike normal cats, I don't have an aversion to taking human baths." He licked his paw and rubbed it over his ear. "Instead of being grateful for the company in his royal chambers, he banned me from the palace *again*. But our silly king hasn't figured out that forbidding me from entering only makes me want to come in more."

"You are a cat, after all," I said. I couldn't resist reaching up to pet him as he stood on my shoulder. His colorful fur was softer than any animal I had petted in my life. I blushed once I realized what I had done. "I'm so sorry!"

"Since you are our Alice, I shall allow it." He nuzzled against my cheek with a purr as I petted him again. "It is wonderful to have you back, dear friend.

I've been dreadfully lonely without you and your magic to entertain me."

Bianco sighed as he gave in to the inevitable. "Bad things happen when you're left to entertain yourself."

"They would be very good if our ruler wasn't so uptight. We used to have great fun together before him taking the throne ruined everything." Cheshire gave a disdainful sniff. "It's quite rude that he doesn't appreciate my efforts to help him enjoy himself like his princely days."

"The crown is a heavy burden to bear," Bianco said with a sympathetic expression. "King Rei is doing the best he can to make Wonderland into the great kingdom it once was."

"Perhaps I should teach him a lesson by stealing his crown again," Cheshire declared. "Then he can finally be my Rei like he used to be every day."

I wasn't sure if I should ask, but I was dying to know. "Did you used to be his boyfriend?"

"What a curious term. I have always been a boy and a friend to him." Cheshire gave a purring chuckle that made me laugh. "The King of Hearts belongs to his kingdom and people, but Rei is *mine*."

"He would beg to differ," Bianco said with an amused snort.

"Well, he's very welcome to beg me for forgiveness." Cheshire gave a haughty sniff. "If I am in a magnanimous mood, perhaps I shall reward him for his good behavior."

Bianco merely shook his head as we continued to chat on the way to the palace.

Time passed as we continued our journey. It was a beautiful day for a walk, especially when Bianco and Cheshire were wonderful company. The real world and the fundraiser felt a million light-years away. Although the prospect of being the hero of Wonderland was scary, at least I didn't have to go to war like the original Alice did when she returned. I had no choice but to trust Bianco's assertions that no harm would come to me when he released the magic within me that I still wasn't convinced I possessed.

"Would you be so kind as to pretend I'm not here?" Cheshire murmured in my ear as we neared the palace walls. "It will make it more fun to surprise Our Majesty."

I turned to glance at him, just in time to watch him disappear into nothingness. While I couldn't see him anymore, I could still feel the weight of his cat form as he continued riding on my shoulder. I answered him with a simple nod.

Cheshire rewarded me with a nuzzle on my cheek.

"What a wonderful and kind Alice you are, Alistair. Bianco chose well."

It wasn't until we passed through the gates that I got my first real look at the massive Palace of Hearts. Everything was a gleaming white that sparkled in the sunlight, with heart-shaped stained-glass windows. It drove home that despite the impossibility of it all, I had somehow entered a magical fairy-tale land.

My stomach churned with anxiety over the thought of meeting royalty for the first time in my life. The odds I would fuck it up were as high as Vivalter's smoke made me feel. "Are there any court rules I need to be aware of when I meet the king?" I asked Bianco. "I don't want to offend him by doing something wrong."

"A simple bow when you first meet him and addressing him as 'Your Majesty' is all you need to do."

I frowned at the answer. "That doesn't seem like enough."

"King Rei doesn't care for formalities, so he's not much for pomp and circumstance. You needn't worry. While he is reticent, he is kind at heart."

"But truth be told, he's a bit of a grumpy cat," Cheshire whispered in my ear, making it very difficult to not laugh out loud. "He's all growl and no bite, though."

If nothing else, I was grateful Bianco had picked me up at a formal event when I was in dress clothes. Thankfully, I was wearing a red jacket, which was the official color of the kingdom. It would have mortified me to meet a king in my normal jeans and hoodie or in a blue suit. I tried to settle my nerves, but it was hard when I was so far out of my element.

"Don't worry, dear Alistair. If our king is in a grouchy mood, I shall do my part to make everything better. You have nothing to fear." Cheshire's soft purring helped calm me.

I tried to trust in their reassurances as Bianco led us through a winding maze of endless hallways and corridors that left me dizzy. The extravagance of royal luxury put the event space I had been in earlier to shame. I was in awe as we passed countless objects of art that I would have loved to inspect if we had the time. The scale of everything was so massive, it was like I had shrunk down again and was three inches tall.

Bianco stopped outside two massive doors that had ornate golden filigree hearts on them. There were guards standing on either side in red-and-white uniforms, holding giant spears crossed in front of the doors. They moved their weapons away from the door and banged them against the floor three times in unison.

The doors swung open, revealing a massive room that was filled with the kaleidoscope of colors filtering in from the floor-to-ceiling stained-glass windows. A red carpet with golden edges ran down the center aisle, leading to a cherrywood throne that had a heart-shaped back.

I shied away from the sight of King Rei of Hearts sitting on it, but Bianco nudged me forward to keep walking. As I walked down the absurdly long carpet, I kept repeating to myself like a mantra: *don't fuck it up, don't trip and fall, don't show your whole ass in front of this ridiculously handsome king.*

The ruler appeared to be in his late twenties or early thirties, with fire-red hair that fell in waves around him. The gold crown on his head had red rubies in the shape of hearts encircling it. Combined with his luxurious red tunic embellished with gold thread and white pants, the man was the picture of elegant, royal refinement.

Once we got closer, I noticed his striking eyes, which were as red as the bright rubies in his crown. Despite his relative youth, there was an air of weariness around him as he watched us approach with an apathetic gaze. He looked like a royal who had seen some shit and was over it all, which was honestly a mood. Hopefully, he didn't share the "off with their head" mentality of the Queen of Hearts in the books.

Bianco stopped in front of King Rei, giving a formal bow as he greeted him. "I have returned, Your Majesty."

I froze as I tried to figure out how I was supposed to bow when I still had an invisible cat on my shoulder. In my momentary panic, I gave an awkward curtsy instead, causing one of the king's red eyebrows to arch in judgment. Cheshire vibrated with what I assumed was silent laughter, bringing heat to my cheeks as I gazed at the stairs below the king's feet and tried not to die of embarrassment. So much for not fucking it up and showing my whole ass in front of royalty. But at least I didn't fall? Then again, maybe it was too early to celebrate that. I still had to walk out of the room first.

"After searching long and hard, I have finally found our missing Alice," Bianco said, gesturing to me. "May I present Alistair Hargreaves, Your Majesty."

"So, *this* is Alice?" King Rei asked in a deep baritone voice. The slight hint of a British accent made him even hotter. Why was everyone in Wonderland so outrageously attractive? Or was I just *that* horny? "Are you quite certain of it?"

Bianco bowed his head. "Without a doubt, Alistair is the Alice we have been searching for, Your Majesty."

"I'm not convinced. This boy lacks the muchness of Alice that I have heard so many tales of."

On the one hand, part of me was offended at his dismissive assessment. On the other, I completely agreed with his skepticism. There was no way in hell I was qualified to be the savior of Wonderland. But the disapproval still burned. It was bad enough that I was judged as a fuck-up in the real world, but did it have to be true in Wonderland, too? Bianco and Cheshire's reactions had almost made me believe I could do the impossible task ahead of me.

Cheshire caressed my neck with his tail in silent comfort. The show of support took some of the sting out of the king's words.

"I assure you, I can sense the magic deep inside his soul. There is no mistake. This is our Alice. He's our only hope of recovering Wonderland's long-lost glory. Vivalter has also confirmed that Alistair is indeed the Alice I've been searching for all this time."

Although my heart hammered with nervousness, I dared to glance up. My breathing hitched when my gaze met the king's. The man was strikingly handsome, even with a slight frown of disapproval on his face as he studied me.

"And what do you have to say for yourself, Alice?" King Rei asked.

I swallowed the urge to correct him about my name as I rallied myself to answer the ruler. "It is a pleasure to meet you, Your Majesty." I hated how my voice trembled with nerves.

He continued to seem unimpressed with me. "Are you prepared to do whatever it takes to restore Wonderland's magic?"

I wasn't about to admit that I was totally in over my head and was more likely to fuck up things further than pull off such an incredible feat. Instead, I simply nodded. "Yes, Your Majesty. I'll do anything Bianco tells me." *Especially in the bedroom*, I accidentally added before checking myself. Those were not thoughts to have in front of a sexy king.

He remained unconvinced. "You are not to leave Wonderland until you restore the magic to these lands."

My concern wasn't that I couldn't leave; it was that I didn't *want* to. I swallowed hard as I wondered how long it would take Bianco to work what seemed like an impossible miracle to me. What if they sent me home after they were done with me? How the fuck was I supposed to return to a normal life after being in Wonderland?

Before I could find the wherewithal to answer him or spiral out further, Cheshire jumped off my shoulder. "You should be kinder to our Alice, Rei. He's come a terribly long way to help us."

The king stiffened in his seat as his eyes scanned the room for the source of the voice. "Cheshire!"

The cat shifter materialized in his human form, sitting on King Rei's lap with his legs draped over the throne chair arm. He reached up and daringly ran his fingers through the king's long hair, shocking me with his forwardness. "At your service."

Rather than getting angry, King Rei's expression became sensual. "Does that mean you'd be willing to do absolutely anything for me?"

Cheshire brought strands of the ruler's hair to his lips to press a reverent kiss on them. "I live to take care of *all* your needs."

"Then go away," King Rei said in a sultry tone that made my jaw drop at the sudden reversal.

The cat shifter reached up to cup the king's cheek in his hand, caressing him with his thumb. "I will if you give me a goodbye kiss." He leaned in until their lips were a breath away from touching. "Please, Rei." There was a genuine longing in his voice that broke my heart, although I knew nothing about their clearly compli-cated relationship.

King Rei hesitated for a moment, almost like he was thinking about doing what Cheshire asked. But he drew back to demand in a frustrated tone, "Why do you always ask for things you know I can't do?"

"Contrariwise, I have firsthand knowledge that you can give *excellent* goodbye kisses, along with hello, passionate, ardent, sexy, demanding, and tender ones, too," Cheshire retorted with his famous grin. "If you're worried about being out of practice, I'd be happy to help you brush up on your skills."

"That won't be necessary."

Instead of being deterred, Cheshire reached up and tugged Rei down for a needy kiss that was a welcome deposit in my spank bank to enjoy later when I was alone. King Rei gave in to the hunger as he gave it back as good as he got it before he pulled away with an aggrieved sigh. "Did you forget that it's stunts like that which keep getting you banned from the palace?"

"I didn't forget. I just don't care." His grin turned

impish. "Now, why don't you take me to your room and punish me with your royal rod to teach me a sexy lesson?"

I had to stifle a laugh because I was pretty sure cracking up at the euphemism would get me in trouble. Even if King Rei didn't have the same "off with their heads" mentality as his predecessor, I didn't want to risk incurring his wrath within minutes of meeting the man.

King Rei constrained himself to a mere eye roll. "If I thought it was a lesson you would learn, I might actually consider it."

Cheshire sighed in disappointment. "Very well. You leave with me no choice, then." Before the king could ask what he meant, the cat shifter stole his crown and moved with an alacrity befitting of his feline heritage. "If you want this back, you'll have to get naked and come play with me in your bed as you beg for forgiveness. But don't take too long. If I get bored, who knows when you'll see this again?" He twirled it around on his finger for emphasis.

"Stay out of my bedro—" Before King Rei could finish his sentence, Cheshire and the crown both disappeared in the blink of an eye. The door to the room opened by itself and slammed with a finality that made the ruler flinch.

The royal closed his eyes with a weary sigh as he rubbed his hand over his face and took a moment to collect himself. "I swear to all the gods above, someday, I will rid myself of that menace for good."

"You know he means well," Bianco said in a gentle tone, making me wonder how often he had to play the intermediary between the two men.

"I'm not sure which is worse: him refusing to leave me alone or me always giving in to him before I regain control of my senses." There was so much frustration in his words that I couldn't help but feel bad for him.

"Perhaps if you would forego the regaining control of your senses part, your life would be far less stressful," Bianco suggested.

King Rei pinned his mage under his disapproving gaze. "We both know damn well that getting his way only makes him more incorrigible. You, of all people, understand the reasons why that's not an option for me."

"And you know why I think those reasons are convenient excuses not to give in to what you want. Given our present company, I will skip our normal banter on the subject and merely suggest you go upstairs before it's too late and you lose yet *another* crown. If you run out of them, he'll argue you're no longer king and can be with him once again."

Another tired sigh escaped from the king. "And how many am I down to now?"

"Counting this one? Four."

"*Great.*" King Rei stood up, startling me at how tall

he was. Maybe it would be worth it to nibble a little more of the Eat Me cake in my pocket to even things out since everyone was stupid tall in Wonderland. "It seems I have no choice but to go deal with the menace before I have to get the crown jeweler to make me new ones."

"In that case, I will take Alistair and get him settled in his room. I'll update you on the situation once he's had some time to get comfortable." Bianco gestured for me to follow him.

Since I didn't have Cheshire to worry about, I gave a deep formal bow to the king before I hurried after Bianco out of the throne room. It was impossible not to feel bad for the King of Hearts, who ironically wasn't allowed to follow his to Cheshire as he so obviously desired.

Well, looking on the bright side, at least no one expected me to fall in love with the king and become the new Queen of Hearts. I had dodged a bullet when that position seemed to belong solely to Cheshire, despite the king's protests to the contrary. But I wasn't opposed to the idea of falling in love while being their Alice. Maybe I'd have better luck in Wonderland than I did with all the shitbag men back in the real world.

CHAPTER
SIX
BIANCO

After leaving the throne room, Alistair seemed nervous as we walked through the winding corridors.

"What's wrong?" I asked.

He didn't answer immediately. "Am I going to get in trouble?"

"In trouble for what?"

He glanced around to make sure there was nobody nearby to overhear. "For sneaking Cheshire into the palace. But in my defense, I didn't know *that* would happen with the king."

I chuckled at his innocent question. "You have nothing to worry about. I was well aware of the situation."

He looked at me in surprise. "Then why didn't you stop it?"

"The short answer is because Cheshire does whatever he wants." I laughed as I continued leading Alistair through the winding palace maze. "Don't you know you can't tell a cat what to do?"

That drew a chuckle from him. "That's true. What's the long answer?"

"That's best saved for when we're alone in your room to discuss." It was not something I'd ever address in public with a risk of being overheard.

He perked up. "Is that where we're headed?"

I nodded. "It is. We're almost there."

"How am I ever going to learn the layout of the palace?" He glanced around with a groan. "This place is *enormous*."

"Don't worry. I'll help you find your way."

He scoffed. "Good luck. My sense of direction is *awful*."

"Luckily, I have a few tricks up my sleeve that should help." I chuckled as I let us into his room. "Here's where you'll be staying."

Alistair looked around the massive chambers with an awed expression. They were furnished with the best comforts the kingdom could offer a guest of the king. Everything was decorated with red velvet and dark woods gilded with gold.

As he continued exploring, I told him about the history of the space. "This was the room Alice once stayed in during her time here. Because of that, this area still possesses the old palace magic. I believe you will find it very helpful during your stay."

His expression turned curious. "What do you mean?"

I gestured for him to join me at the long dining table. "Twinkle, please set the table to have tea for two."

At my request, the table shrank to a smaller round one, more convenient for conversing with a friend. A teapot, teacups, and food fit for a tea party appeared, causing Alistair to exclaim a colorful expletive in surprise.

"While in your suite here, you can make any request by asking Twinkle. Unfortunately, this magic has been lost to the rest of the palace." I was determined to restore Wonderland to its former magical glory, though. "Please, take a seat. Thank you for this lovely spread, Twinkle."

Alistair sat across from me. "Who is Twinkle?"

"Twinkle is the magic itself." I poured us both a cup of steaming hot tea. "Alice had a wonderfully creative imagination. She enjoyed thinking that a friendly sprite named Twinkle would make all her dreams come true whenever she asked. Apparently, the magic grew to love that, so it will only respond in this room if you refer to it as Alice once did."

Alistair picked up the delicate teacup that had a red heart motif on it, blowing on the piping hot tea. "That's sweet that she would treat the magic like a person."

"It's funny. I found it so odd when she first started doing it, but now, Twinkle is an old friend who brings me great comfort whenever I visit." I smiled when the magic in the room seemed to ripple with happiness at my words. "You will soon learn that Twinkle can be a wonderful companion, especially if you have proper manners, as Alice once did."

"Then we should get along nicely, unless it gets upset about occasional swearing." He gave me a wicked grin that made me laugh. "What pronouns did Alice use for Twinkle? I want to be respectful, and calling the magic 'it' seems quite rude."

He was quite right. "Very true. Alice pictured Twinkle as a boy fairy who would dance on dust motes in the sunlight."

"It's very nice to make your acquaintance, Twinkle. Thank you for taking care of me." He pointed to the tray of snacks. "What are these?"

"Some of Alice's favorite tea party treats. They're mostly different cakes and tarts since she had quite a sweet tooth."

He lit up with excitement. "Then it seems I have more in common with Alice than I thought." He picked up a dewberry cake and put it on his plate. When he got his first taste, he moaned in delight in a way that gave the naughty part of me bad thoughts. "Twinkle, that's so delicious! Oh, I could get *very* used to this."

I could feel the magic almost preen with pride.

"Twinkle is very pleased to hear that you enjoy his work."

Alistair took another bite as he looked at me with curiosity. "How can you tell?"

"Magic is something that touches the core of your soul. It's the most expressive part of a person, so strong feelings come across clearly. I can sense Twinkle's happiness in his bright aura." I could also feel Alistair's magic calling to me, begging me to free it. It was a siren song when combined with his pleasing pheromones that were teasing my senses, spurred on by the memories of how he tasted better than even the best dessert.

"Fascinating." He tried another piece of cake and once again made a sound of delight that caused my prick to stir in the confines of my pants. My beast urged me to encourage him to make more noises like that. It was a most disconcerting reaction. "Twinkle's going to spoil me, isn't he?"

"Quite possibly. He's been terribly lonely without Alice to keep him company. Only Cheshire and I visit Twinkle these days."

My answer seemed to surprise him. "Cheshire comes to see Twinkle?"

"With some amount of regularity, actually. I doubt that will stop now that you're here." I shook my head. "If anything, I expect him to visit even more because of that, so prepare yourself."

"But won't he get in trouble for being here?" He

frowned with concern. "It seems like the king kinda has it out for him. What's their story, anyway?"

"Theirs is a tale with a great deal of history that complicates things." I figured I might as well start from the beginning. Maybe it would take my mind off how tempting Alistair was to me and help me quit remembering how perfect his lips molded against mine as he gave in to me with a moan of pleasure. "King Rei was the third son, so there was never any expectation for him to take the throne. Because of that, he grew up with more freedom compared to the heir and the spare, so to speak."

"What happened?"

I took a bite of cake before I continued the story. "Rex was the eldest. Unfortunately, he inherited the former Queen of Hearts' side of the madness. He was tempestuous, abrasive, and unbearably arrogant about becoming king. Everyone lived in fear of the day he would become ruler, terrified that he'd continue the terrible 'off with their heads' reign of his mother."

Alistair cringed with sympathy. "That sounds horrible."

"Rex's foul temper was legendary throughout the lands. But during the Magic Wars, he challenged a prince from the Kingdom of Diamonds to a duel. While he was a formidable fighter, he lost the battle and paid for his arrogance with his life. Immediately afterward, the tyrannical former Queen of Hearts was assassinated, and her husband fled into exile, ending the war. There was much rejoicing by the people upon finding out those two could no longer terrorize the masses and the fighting was over."

"That must have been awful for their family to see people celebrating their death."

I made an uncertain noise. "While none of them would admit it, it was a relief for them to be free of their tyranny as well. The queen and Rex were out of control. Nobody could stop their cruelty."

Alistair tactfully let the subject of Rex drop. "So, what happened?"

"The second son became the new King of Hearts. However, Regan was more dormouse than man. The only thing he had feared more than Rex's reign was having to be king himself. His nerves couldn't handle the pressure of the crown and rebuilding the country. Shortly afterward, he had a nervous breakdown and renounced his claim on the throne to become a monk, much to the dismay of Rei."

"So, Rei became the ruler by default. No wonder he looked so fucking miserable when we first got there," Alistair said with sympathy.

"He enjoyed living his life untouched by the shadows of the crown, so to have it unexpectedly foisted upon him was a massive burden. The consequences of having to take the throne still weigh heavily on him to this day." As Rei's friend, it was tough to stand by the sidelines and watch, unable to do anything other than support him through it all. "Because of his family's legacy of selfish brutality, he has had to work very hard to prove himself to be a benevolent ruler to win back the people's trust."

"How does Cheshire fit into all of this?"

I tried to find a tactful way of explaining. "When Rei was just a prince, they were lovers for a long time. However, once Rei became king, he broke things off between them."

"But why?" Alistair seemed genuinely upset by the news. It was touching to see.

"Cheshire, Vivalter, March, and I are the only shifters left in the entirety of Wonderland who can freely use magic because of our connection to the original Alice. Over the generations, people have developed a deep distrust of us because of that."

"Why? That should be celebrated, not scorned."

I sighed with a hint of my weariness. "People fear what they do not understand. I hold a certain level of respect due to my long-held position as the king's Private Secretary and Chief Mage, plus I have a stellar record for using my powers for the sake of protecting their beloved ruler. Vivalter also has a respected reputation because of his role as the royal seer. Most people have forgotten about March since he's very good about staying out of the spotlight and never using his abilities in public. But Cheshire is different."

"Why?"

"He flaunts his unique magic and freely shifts between forms. He is an agent of chaos and has made himself quite a spectacle by being a nuisance at court. Stories about him quickly turn into legends, so he is a feared figure throughout the kingdom, even though he would never cause real harm to anyone with his magic."

Alistair took a sip of his tea. "Cheshire is internationally famous in my world, but no one is scared of him. Then again, they don't think he's real, so that probably doesn't mean much."

The issue was a bit more complicated than that. "With his terrible reputation, Cheshire would be a controversial choice for the king's consort. King Rei believes it would put his reign in danger by making people fear him turning into his cruel mother. When he doesn't have an heir, that's a risk he's unwilling to take."

Alistair sipped his tea as he studied me. It seemed like his blue eyes could pierce right through me and see the truth of how much I wanted him. What was going on with me? "But you disagree."

It appeared he was as astute an observer as the original Alice once was. "I do. If given the chance, Cheshire would charm the entire world to be with Rei. People seeing their beloved ruler tame Wonderland's most mysterious magical creature would only add to the list of King Rei's impressive accomplishments. And when we free your magic, it will return to the lands, so

Cheshire would be one of the many once again. Nobody could hold that against him anymore."

"Have you been searching for me because you want to free King Rei to be with Cheshire?"

"I'd be lying if I said that wasn't a major factor in my rush to rediscover our missing Alice." I sighed as I felt for my friends stuck in such an untenable situation. "They're meant to be together, but Rei is just as stubborn as Cheshire sometimes, so he's fighting his feelings because he believes it's for the best of the kingdom."

Alistair frowned. "How is having a miserable king who can't love someone for the best?"

It warmed my heart that he understood the situation so well. "Exactly. But after the former Queen of Hearts' and Rex's awful selfishness, Rei never wants to be seen as a ruler who prioritizes his own needs. Cheshire will never give up until he gets what he wants. The push and pull between what Rei wants and what he thinks he should do for the kingdom is an exhausting game he feels like he can never win. Telling Cheshire no rips his heart apart, but it would hurt even more if Cheshire gave up on him."

Tears gathered in Alistair's eyes. "That's awful."

"It's truly heartbreaking. I struggle with sitting by the sidelines and doing nothing. Speaking of which, I should probably go check on them. If you'll excuse me, I'll return once you've had some time to rest."

"Good luck."

I would certainly need it. Pulling myself away from Alistair was the worst kind of hell, but I had responsibilities to my friends.

K ing Rei didn't look up as I entered his private chambers. He was stretched out on the red velvet chaise by the heart-shaped fireplace, blankly staring at the flames.

I sat down on the nearby armchair. "Is it safe to assume we're down to three crowns now?" I asked in a teasing tone to lighten the mood. There had once been fourteen of them, but Cheshire had a habit of stealing one whenever the stubborn ruler refused to give in to his wishes.

King Rei draped his arm over his head as he looked at me. "Is it bad that I sometimes wish he'd take all of them? Maybe then I wouldn't have to be king anymore."

"But being king is the exact thing that gives you the freedom to define the rules that would allow you to be with Cheshire," I pointed out, and not for the first time.

He was silent for a long moment before he scowled. "I wonder if I will run out of crowns or the willpower to resist him first?"

"My bet is on willpower, personally." I chuckled as he glared at me. "Cheshire is entirely too charming for you to continue resisting."

He groaned as he pressed his hand to his forehead. "And he knows that, too."

"Respectfully, it seems the only one who doesn't is you, Your Majesty."

He scoffed. "Oh, I know all too well, trust me. It's getting harder and harder to resist his advances. Every time he steals a kiss, it reminds me I need him so much I can barely breathe when he's not here. And yet I'm always vexed whenever he's around."

"It is not the fact that he is around that is vexing. It is that he is offering you what you are too afraid to accept. Don't you think it's time to quit this farce of resistance?"

Rather than responding to my question, he pivoted. "How long do you think it'll take you to free the magic inside of Alice?"

I shrugged. "I'm not sure. He clearly has some familiarity with our world from the books. And he's already developed a fondness for Cheshire, so I can't imagine it will take him long to bond with Wonderland."

King Rei stiffened at the mention of his former lover. "What do you mean he has developed a fondness for that damn cat?"

I continued playing up the situation in the hopes it would help get my friend out of his rut. "Cheshire seemed quite charmed by our new Alice when we ran into him on our journey here."

"*That's* why he was here today?" King Rei looked

downright murderous at the thought. "I swear, I'm going to banish that cat from my lands forever."

We both knew it was an empty threat. I pointed out the obvious to distract him. "I'm sure Alistair's appearance was merely a convenient excuse to proposition you once more. Perhaps he hoped that the discovery of Alice would change your mind about being together."

"What difference would that make?"

It wasn't the question I had expected. "Because once I free Alice's magic to return to Wonderland, it will become commonplace once more. People can't object to Cheshire when there are more shifters like us again."

"There are plenty of other reasons for them to not approve of him."

"If you love him, then they will, too." I stood up to leave since I had made all the progress I could for the day. "Do you need anything before I help Alistair get more settled in?"

"No, but thanks." He sat up to face me, running his fingers through his beautiful hair. "I will meet with Alistair tomorrow morning for breakfast since I regrettably didn't make the best impression today because of that vexing nuisance."

I bowed my head in acknowledgment. "Of course. I shall prepare him for it when you're ready."

Before that, I had other things to take care of first.

Instead of returning to Alistair as I had told the king, I had one more stop to make. I went to my room, where Cheshire was waiting for me. He was lying on the couch, holding the crown between his front paws while kicking it with his hind ones. To show his displeasure, he chewed on one of the decorative tips.

When I came closer, Cheshire guarded his prize. "If you're here to take this from me, you'll have to fight me for it."

"You should know I have no intention of fighting you over a crown or anything else." I sat beside him. Although I knew the answer, I said, "Based on that, I'm guessing your encounter with King Rei didn't go the way you wanted it to."

"If it did, I wouldn't be here." Cheshire kicked the crown to the other side of the couch before he sat on my lap with a plaintive cry that broke my heart all over again for my friends. "Why must he torture me by always saying no?"

I gave him a comforting scritch behind the ears. "You know it's because he thinks he's saving you from the people's disapproval by rejecting you."

Cheshire butted his head against my hand in a bid for more pets. "How does that foolish king not understand I am strong enough to stand by his side, no matter what?"

"Because he's as stubborn as you." I smiled down at

Cheshire. "It's one of the main reasons you're perfect for each other. You know I remind him of that every chance I get."

"You're a good friend, Bianco." Cheshire nuzzled against my chin before he shifted into his human form, sprawled out on my lap like the indulgent cat he was. He rested his head against my shoulder as I held him, the same way I did after every fight he had with his mate. "If Rei loved me even half as much as you, I'd be the luckiest person in the world."

"He loves you and only you. That is as true now as it has always been."

"If he truly loved me, he'd be with me." Cheshire sulked with a heavy sigh. "Do you know how much it hurts for your mate to kiss you and then reject you every single time he sees you? It's *agony*."

"King Rei clearly senses that bond between you, but he doesn't understand it because you've never explained it to him. When the other shifters disappeared with the magic, their mating rituals were forgotten about, too. You can't expect him to just *know*."

Cheshire pulled back to give me a rare serious look. "You know why I can't tell him. If I told him he was fated to love me and only me as my eternal mate, he'd feel trapped and reject me for good. I want him to be with me because *he* loves me, not because of our bond."

I ruffled his hair fondly. "Which is why I've never said anything to him about it. But you eventually need to tell him. If you don't, he'll feel betrayed when he finds out."

Cheshire looked down with a sad expression. "It's like I'll lose him no matter what I do. If I tell him that he was born to be my mate, he'll reject me for manipulating him. If I don't tell him he was fated to be mine, he'll reject me for lying to him. What do I do, Bianco?" He buried his face against my neck with a frustrated sigh.

I hugged my friend tightly. "You trust in your mate that he will always love you, no matter what. Fate made him yours. He can't resist that pull of attraction forever. I know you'll be together and happy again." Whatever I needed to do to make it happen, I was willing to do for my friends to love freely once more. "For what it's worth, I think you're finally wearing him down."

Cheshire nuzzled my cheek before giving me a fond smile. "I'll make a wish that your mate is more accepting than mine. Maybe our dear Twinkle can help make that magic happen."

His shift in conversation confused me. "My mate? What are you talking about? I've never had one."

"How curious. You don't feel the least bit different?"

Color crept into my cheek as I thought about the lust that had overtaken me once I had Alistair alone earlier in the library. That had certainly been a new experience. But I feigned ignorance. "No. Why would I?"

"Gee, whatever could have changed?" He gave me his famous grin before he faded into his cat form. "Curiouser and curiouser. Oh, this shall be great fun for me, indeed." With those words, he disappeared, taking the crown with him for his private collection.

As I was left alone in the silence, my confusion mounted. He wasn't talking about Alistair, was he? Surely not. The prophecy would have told me if that were true...right?

CHAPTER
SEVEN
ALISTAIR

Once Bianco left, the first thing I did was take another nibble of the Eat Me cake to gain a few more inches. It was only fair to even out the absurd height difference between me and all the people I had met in Wonderland so far. I didn't need to be taller than them, but I at least wanted to be in the same stratosphere.

After that, I took my time exploring my new space. The bedroom and bathroom were the largest I had ever seen in person. They dwarfed my crappy studio apartment, which was barely larger than a prison cell and about as warm and welcoming as one.

The bed was big enough to have an orgy on, which was probably a weird first thought to have. My second one about how it looked so soft and inviting that I wanted to go to sleep was much more appropriate. I wasn't sure how long Bianco planned on being gone, but he *had* insisted that I take the time to rest. That meant an afternoon nap was definitely in order.

Loosening my tie, I went over to the wardrobe to see if there was something for me to change into. To my great disappointment, it was empty. It seemed like the height of rudeness to sleep naked in a world based on a children's book, so I resolved to stay in my clothes before I remembered to ask for help. "Twinkle, do you have anything more comfortable for me to sleep in?"

A red silk pajama set materialized on my bedsheets. It was a lot fancier than my normal sweats and a T-shirt I lounged around in my apartment, but it looked divine compared to my stiff suit.

"Thanks, Twinkle. I appreciate that." I was a little self-conscious about stripping down in front of the omnipresent magic.

Despite my discomfort, I took a sneak peek in my briefs at my dick to see if my extra inches on my height worked there as well. To my great delight, it was longer and thicker than before, which made me give an internal cheer. *Thank you, Wonderland!*

I wanted to get hard and jerk off to test out the change, but it didn't seem like an opportune time to do so when a servant might check up on me next. The last thing I needed was someone walking in on me while I was testing out my newly improved dick.

Instead of enjoying my good fortune, I put on the

silk pajamas. I sighed in pleasure at how soft the fabric was against my skin. Damn, I could get used to being treated like royalty. "Wow, this is seriously the nicest thing I've ever worn."

I hung my clothes in the wardrobe before burrowing under the luxurious sheets. All my stress over the bizarre situation I found myself in melted away as I relaxed into the comfort of the bed.

To my surprise, the room darkened. I realized that Twinkle must have somehow tinted the windows to make it easier for me to rest during the sunny afternoon. "You're the best, Twinkle. That was very considerate of you." It had been a long time since somebody had taken such good care of me.

While I once again contemplated jerking off to thoughts about how sexy my encounter with Bianco had been in the library, my exhaustion from the walk in the forest caught up to me. I quickly dropped off into a dreamless sleep.

I gradually realized someone was speaking. "What do you think of our new Alice, Twinkle?" There was a long pause. "Yes, I agree. I believe he will do quite nicely, too. Bianco is one lucky rabbit. It's terribly exciting to have a new playmate again, isn't it?"

Blinking away the sleep, I opened my eyes. The

lights slowly came up, revealing Cheshire sitting on the bed in his cat form, regarding me with a curious head tilt. "Are you allowed to be here?" I asked in a groggy voice as I rolled onto my side to face him.

"I'm a cat who does as he pleases." To prove his point, he walked over and curled up against my chest. "Besides, an afternoon catnap generally requires a cat."

Without thinking, I brought my arm up to pet him. "Oh, sorry, I shouldn't have—"

"You're also allowed to do as you please." He butted his head against my hand in a not-so-subtle hint. "Especially when it pleases me, too."

I hesitantly pet him again, earning me a loud purr as he snuggled closer. "The king won't cut off my head because you're in my bed, will he?"

"The only person he should be mad at is himself. He's welcome to pet me in bed himself, anytime His Royal Majesty pleases. He just chooses not to." Cheshire harrumphed with displeasure. "Perhaps when your magic returns to Wonderland, we'll discover he's secretly a cat shifter. It would certainly explain a lot. And then, he'd have no reason to refuse me anymore."

I continued petting Cheshire, enjoying the experience, although it was extraordinarily weird to do it when I knew there was a man somewhere inside him. "I hope Bianco can unseal the magic in me soon so you can be with the king again. It's too sad that you're not allowed to be together."

"It's hard to love from afar. But it would be far harder not to love him at all," he said in a sad voice that broke my heart. "What about you, dear Alistair? Who do you love?"

"The wrong guy, every single time." I huffed with a bitter laugh. "But it's my fault for always picking someone who doesn't love me back."

He nuzzled under my chin in comfort. "So, you don't believe in fated mates?"

"You mean soul mates?" I shrugged. "The idea that there's one person out there destined to love you forever is comforting, I guess. But all my experience has told me that person doesn't exist. The world isn't nearly that kind to me. It's given me a big middle finger and told me I'm going to die alone."

"Perhaps where you come from is bereft of good choices. But Wonderland is a very different place."

"But I eventually have to go back home, don't I?" The thought of returning to my depressing, lonely life was crushing.

Cheshire's purr was reassuring. "Not according to me. I think you should stay here forever."

It was an odd assertion. "Why? You've only just met me."

"I've known your soul in two lifetimes as one of my dearest and truest friends. Your form may have changed, but your heart is still as pure and full of love as dear old Alice's. I don't wish to be parted from you again, so I do hope you'll stay. It's so lonely when I don't have my favorite Alice to keep me company."

I patted Cheshire. "It sounds pathetic, but I have no reason to go home. No family, no real friends, no partner of any kind, no pets. Hell, I don't even have *plants*. All I have is laundry and an empty bachelor's fridge. And I *hate* my shitty desk job and awful coworkers at my toxic financial firm."

"Then it sounds like you have every reason to stay here with us, your real friends." His purring grew louder. "It will thrill Bianco to hear that."

I could feel my cheeks heating up at the mere thought of the beautiful man who made my heart beat that much faster. "Why him?"

"Because you are very special. Perhaps more than he even realizes yet."

The comment confused me. "In what way?"

"You'll find out soon enough." Cheshire perked up suddenly, his ears swiveling at a sound I couldn't hear. "And here he comes. Is our beloved king still sulking? I sure hope so."

"He's as miserable as you," Bianco said as he entered my room. Every time I saw him, his beauty made my heart stutter in my chest as I forgot what air was for a moment. "You better hope he never finds you in Alistair's bed. He will be most unforgiving."

"Then he should invite me into his bed instead." Cheshire gave a disdainful sniff. "Besides, what does he have to fear? Alistair-once-Alice is a dear friend. Nobody could accuse me of being untoward with him when I'm here as a cat and not a man."

"Cat form or not, if you think Rei will overlook you being stroked in bed with another man so easily, perhaps you don't know him as well as you think." Bianco chuckled as he sat on the other side of my bed. "I wouldn't advise you try to make him jealous that way. It is more likely to backfire and cause greater harm."

"If he wants me to only sleep in his bed, then he'll have to do something about it, won't he?" Cheshire's tail flicked in irritation. "Such a cowardly cat. It's most unbecoming of a king."

"Do you think he'll turn into a cat shifter when my magic is unsealed?" I asked. The concept fascinated me.

"No, but admittedly, it would be very fitting," Bianco answered. "A shifter has never been a member of the royal family."

"*Yet*," Cheshire added in a pointed tone.

Bianco leaned over to give the cat some soothing pats. "Your time will come. You just need to be patient a little longer."

"But I'm *so* tired of being patient." Cheshire grumbled with discontentment. "Can't we hurry up to the part where he changes his mind?"

"I promise we'll do everything we can to make it happen. But we will need some time for Alistair to get settled before he's ready for what needs to be done."

"You won't need nearly as much time as you think," Cheshire confidently predicted.

Bianco arched an eyebrow in a devastatingly handsome manner. "What makes you so sure?"

"You're you and he is him, which makes all the difference in the world." Cheshire chuckled at his own joke, but he lost me.

It appeared Bianco was as well. "Why?"

"Because no one else will do." Cheshire nuzzled against me before standing up. "Farewell for now. I'll come back to have fun again soon, dearest Alistair, Bianco, and Twinkle." In the blink of an eye, he disappeared.

Bianco sighed softly. "As always, he's a mystery wrapped in a conundrum, leaving more questions than answers. He truly is the maddest cat in all the lands."

"I don't know. He seemed quite sane to me—at least compared to the famous version in literature." I tried not to get too distracted by the realization that I was alone in a bed with Bianco. "He's a lot sweeter than I would have expected."

"Just be careful. King Rei is normally quite rational, but he loses all good sense when it comes to that ornery cat. He will be quick to misunderstand Cheshire's affection for you."

"How did he react when Cheshire was friends with the original Alice?"

"He was an infant back then, so he doesn't

remember her. He only remembers the stories that have been told about her. But even if he remembered Cheshire always keeping watch over her, it would be different with you."

It wasn't hard to read between the lines. "Because I'm a man and he would view me as a potential threat?"

Bianco smiled wanly. "I wish I could say otherwise, but King Rei acts before he thinks regarding their troublesome relationship. He refuses to be with Cheshire, but he can't bear the thought of anyone else being with him, either."

I frowned at that. "But how is that fair to Cheshire?"

"It's not, but that doesn't matter. Cheshire is devoted to his beloved, and nothing will sway him away. His heart and soul belong to him, even if King Rei refuses to take good care of him the way he should." Bianco shifted on the bed with a sigh, making my dick perk up with interest. "While Cheshire is only in love with the king, he is a friendly cat who loves freely and is overly affectionate. It has caused enough problems in the past that I know better than to promise you it will be fine in the future."

"I'll do what I can to not antagonize the king." I pulled the covers tighter around me to hide the fact I was getting hard again from being so close to Bianco. But I couldn't help it! There was something about him that got me all stirred up inside. "But it was nice spending time with Cheshire, so I'll be sad if I can't see him again."

Bianco's expression was sympathetic. "As I said earlier, Cheshire will visit often, even though it displeases the king."

"It's understandable. It was totally platonic, but from his perspective, I would still be in bed with his boyfriend, so I would understand why he'd be pissed off."

"Well, that, and Cheshire is likely to antagonize him further by taking their game too far. Let's hope things do not reach that point, though."

Since I wasn't sure what else to say to that, I switched topics. "So, how does this unlocking my magic thing work? Is there anything I have to do?"

"That will come later. Today has been enough of a whirlwind without that. Let's have a lovely dinner and get to know each other better tonight. Tomorrow, I will take you around the palace grounds and perhaps introduce you to a few people. We can worry about the magic later."

I lit up at the possibilities. "Could I meet the Mad Hatter sometime?"

He smiled at my enthusiastic reaction. "He would be quite put out if you didn't. Hatter's eccentric but far from mad. And he throws the most marvelous tea parties with his friends."

"I'd love to go, even if it wasn't mad."

"That can be arranged." Bianco stood up from the bed. "Twinkle, please provide Alistair with something to wear and prepare dinner for us."

A pair of red pants with a loose-fitting white shirt appeared. That kind of magic would never stop amazing me. "Thank you, Twinkle."

"I'll leave you to change." With that, Bianco walked back into the living room section, shutting the door behind him.

While it was disappointing that we couldn't continue our amorous adventure, I was still excited about having dinner with the White Rabbit I had loved so much as a kid. If it was anything like afternoon tea, I was in for one of the best meals of my life. And maybe if I was *really* lucky, we'd end up in bed together again.

It was cute watching Alistair take such tremendous delight in dinner. There was something charming about his unabashed appreciation of everything that had been done for him so far. It was a relief that he appeared to be excited about his visit to Wonderland and not looking for a way to escape his responsibilities. I had been prepared to do a considerable amount of coaxing to persuade him to stay and help.

Or you could coax him into bed, my beast whispered. I shushed it and did my best to ignore how unruly it had been all day. It was most unusual behavior and a trend I did not care for in the least.

"So, what do you think about the *Alice in Wonderland* books?" Alistair asked as we continued eating dinner. "I'm guessing she must have brought them back with her the second time, if you know about them."

"Correct. While they're full of inaccuracies, I understand why children would be charmed by them. It's hard to hate something that Alice herself loved."

"Was anyone pissed off about how they were represented?"

I chuckled at the question. "Hatter is the only person who objected to his depiction. I can't say that I blame him, though."

Alistair tilted his head as he regarded me with curiosity. "Why?"

"You'll understand why the Mad Hatter is a far cry from reality once you meet him." It would become clear to Alistair quite quickly why Hatter would prefer not to be associated with such an outlandish, old character. "At this point, the books are an oddity that only those of us who were around back then remember. They've been forgotten about in some desolate, dusty corner of the royal library."

"That amazes me when they're still world-famous in my time."

The information surprised me. "Really?" I had assumed he had only been familiar with the books since he was a descendant of Alice.

"Oh, yeah. They've made so many movies, video games, merchandise, and alternative retellings. All of you live on in everyone's imaginations to this day."

"How unexpected." It warmed my heart to know that some part of Alice continued to exist in Alistair's era. "With as much time that has passed, I assumed everyone would have forgotten us."

He shook his head. "Far from it. It's popular all around the world to this day. That's why I can't believe I'm really here."

"If you don't mind me saying, I'm a bit perplexed that you don't seem to be in a hurry to go home."

"Why would I want to live my boring old life when I can have fun in Wonderland?" He scoffed before taking a sip of tea.

The answer surprised me. "But don't you have anyone who will be eager for your return?"

"Nah, my mom was the only person who cared about me, and she died when I was a kid."

I regretted bringing the subject up without more tact. "I am so sorry for your loss."

"She would have been *so* jealous I was here," he said with a wan smile. "*Alice in Wonderland* and *Through the Looking-Glass* were her favorite books. She'd read them to me before bed every night. We would even have tea parties together. She used to say she waited her whole life for the White Rabbit to find her so she could go on a real adventure. That was why she named me Alistair with an *I* instead of A-L-A-S-T-A-I-R, because she wanted me to be the male Alice. I guess she got her wish after all."

"She did." My heart went out to him for losing someone who had loved him so much. "It will be my honor to make her wish come true for you."

His pleased smile was precious. "That would be awesome. But yeah, other than a few mementos I'd like to pick up, I don't have anything worth returning to." He held his hands together in prayer. "Please don't make me go back to the real world after you've freed the magic from me. I seriously have nothing waiting for me there. At least I can be helpful here and people seem to want me around."

"We certainly want you here. Everything will change for the better because of you." I looked forward to the day magic returned to our lands with his help. "But there's no need to rush and release the magic immediately. I'd prefer you to be comfortable during your stay here."

"I've never been more comfortable in my life," he said with a chuckle. "This is like living in the lap of ultimate luxury compared to my tiny studio apartment with a crappy bed. I've already had more fun with you and Cheshire today than I've had in forever. I'm not in any rush for this to end yet."

"We can take our time. It's important for you to feel at home here."

Alistair sat up a little straighter. "Because I have to form a bonding love in my heart for Wonderland to unlock the magic?"

"Exactly."

He worried his lower lip with his teeth. "Are you sure I only have to bond with Wonderland and not a person? That seems odd to me."

"There's no mention of another person in Vivalter's prophecy, so I believe that the 'bonding love in their heart' refers to Wonderland itself rather than a person." It was an issue I had given a great deal of thought to. "Surely, it would speak of forming a bonding love with their true love if it were a romantic one that needed to form."

He still didn't look convinced. "I suppose that makes sense."

"You don't need to put any pressure on yourself. Once you're more settled here, I will test the magical seals inside you and determine what needs to be done." I was curious to see what I would discover, but I didn't want to rush Alistair and make him uncomfortable. "I promise it will be entirely painless."

His apprehension was easy to see. "Even when dealing with the dark magic?"

"Yes, even then. At most, you'll experience a sense of relief once it has been purified, like you've been unburdened at long last."

That seemed to put him at ease. "I think I can handle that."

"You have nothing to worry about, Alistair. I

promise I'll take excellent care of you. No harm shall befall you while you are here."

He fidgeted with his hands. "I guess I have a hard time believing that when, in all the modern adaptations of *Alice in Wonderland*, the dark forces are all out to kill her."

I arched an eyebrow at that piece of information. "Wonderland has not been that kind of dangerous place in centuries. After the dark magic was sealed inside of Alice almost two hundred years ago during the Magic Wars, our world has known peace. You have nothing to fear."

"Um, I don't mean this to sound rude, but how old *are* you?"

His question caused me to chuckle. "King Rei is one hundred and fifty-six. I'll be three hundred and seventeen later this year. Cheshire is four hundred and twenty. Vivalter is six hundred and sixty-nine years old. And Hatter has been around as long as anyone can remember. I don't think even he knows how old he is."

He blinked in astonishment. "But everyone I've met so far looks like they're in their twenties and thirties in human years!"

"Time works differently in Wonderland." I shrugged since it was one of the many great mysteries. "To us, you appear to be in your late one hundreds."

His shock was comical. "Do I at least look good for my age?"

I chuckled at his question. "You are as beautiful as I would have expected our Alice to be." It made it difficult to control myself around him, which was something I had never struggled with before.

"But isn't it weird that I'm a guy?" He gestured to himself to emphasize his maleness. I certainly didn't need the reminder. The memory of how wonderful it had been to have his prick sliding down my throat as I worshipped him made mine harden. "Alice should be a girl, right?"

I tried to ignore my growing arousal. What was it about him that drove me to such madness? "An Alice is less about their gender and more about the qualities that make up their muchness. It's their pure heart, defiant courage, powerful magic, and unwavering belief in the good of people that defines the descendants of an Alice."

"But there have been a *lot* of generations between her and me. Why am *I* the one you chose as your missing Alice?"

"Because your magic called out to me." Even now, it beckoned to me, begging me to merge my power with his as I indulged in sensual explorations of his beautiful body.

He leaned forward with an intrigued expression. "How did it do that?"

"It tugged on a piece of my soul and wouldn't let go until I found you." I pressed my hand over my heart as I remembered the sensation. "As soon as I noticed the first stirrings, I started trying to get back to Overland to find you. It took some time since the weak magic controlling the barriers between our realms made it difficult to reach you. But once I saw you, I knew you were the one I was looking for."

His cheeks grew pink. "I'm glad you found me. And I'm not just saying that because your mouth is a wonderland all unto itself."

I licked my lips as I remembered the taste of him. "While you are kind to say that, it was wrong of me not to show more restraint. Especially when I can tell you are untouched."

He shifted in his chair. A teasing hint of his arousal reached my nose and once again made my beast rattle in its cage. "Are you telling me you can smell that I'm a virgin?"

"Rabbits have incredibly sensitive noses." It was currently a tremendous source of delight as I basked in his tempting scent.

He hid his face in his hands with a pained groan. "What the fractional fuck? Seriously?"

"What are you ashamed of?"

"Because I'm almost thirty and a virgin, which is humiliating." He gestured at me. "And everything about you says masterful fucker who can give untold pleasures to all the partners who are lucky enough to be yours."

I arched my eyebrows at the description. "What a fascinating assessment."

"Where's the lie?"

"I've never had a partner, let alone multiple ones." It was difficult not to laugh at the comical way his jaw dropped. "I am also a virgin, so I see no shame in that."

He spluttered as he turned an interesting shade of pink. "Oh, I call bullshit, sir! You sucked my dick like you had been doing it every day of your life for all the centuries you've been alive. Between your talent and good looks, I'm sure most of the people in this kingdom have thrown themselves at you."

"Contrary to your assumption, I've never had a partner of any kind before." I shrugged as he continued making fractured sounds of disbelief. "That was my first sexual experience with someone, so—"

"*Fucking how?*" Alistair demanded, his voice rising in pitch. He pressed his hand against his forehead as he stared at me in shock. "Please explain to me how somebody who is literally sex on legs and has a mouth that would put a vacuum cleaner to shame has never done *anything* with a person before?"

"I never saw a point in being with a man who wasn't my mate. And since I've never found mine—"

"But you're a *rabbit*, right?" He continued flailing in his shock. "Where I come from, there's a saying about people fucking like bunnies when they go at it all the time. And you're telling me *you've never fucked?*"

I tilted my head as I looked at him. "Why does that seem to distress you so much?"

"Because I can't fathom how somebody as incredible as you hasn't been locked down yet. Or how you could be *that* masterful at giving a blow job your first time."

"My beast was guiding me on instinct." It was gratifying to know I had done so well. "But I don't know what you mean by 'locked down yet.' Do you mean locked up?"

He shook his head. "No, I mean someone as handsome as you and with such a magical mouth should have been claimed by a partner already." His eyebrows furrowed. "Wait, if you've been celibate for almost three hundred and seventeen years, why in the fuck did you decide to rock my world today with the best blow job ever?"

I chose my words carefully. "Everything about you is incredibly appealing, and when combined with the power your magic holds over my beast, I lost control of my senses."

The color crept into his cheeks again. "I don't suppose you want to lose control of your senses again?"

I shuddered as my beast vehemently demanded we accept what was being offered so willingly. But I owed it to Alistair to show restraint. "I shouldn't. It's not fair to you."

"Fuck being fair. Do you want me?"

I clenched my hands into fists to stop them from

reaching out to him. "It would be improper. I don't want you to think I only have an interest in you because my beast is drawn to your magic."

"Here's the thing. We're in Wonderland. It's where everyone is mad, right?" His blue eyes peered deep into my soul. "It's a place where anything can happen."

I couldn't find my voice, so I merely nodded.

"In that case, it's cool with me if your beast wants me for my magic. Honestly, that's hot in its own way. Although I'm not your mate, as long as *you* want me and won't regret it, you can do anything you want to me." Alistair got up and walked over to me. "So, the question is do *you* want me?"

My beast did not have the same sense of decency and decorum as me. It urged me to my feet, pinning Alistair against the table as we stole another passionate kiss. We burned with a need for more, and my beast wasn't stopping until we got another taste of him.

Alistair yelped in surprise when I picked him up and carried him back to the bedroom. "Holy fuck, that's *so* hot!"

Since we weren't in Overland anymore, I was free to use my magic to rid us both of our clothes as soon as we were on the bed. I pinned him down, indulging in more demanding kisses as my beast ran amok within me.

But I had enough presence of mind to notice something important. I reached down to stroke his prick, which had grown since I had enjoyed a taste of him in the library. "It looks like you took advantage of a slice of Eat Me cake while we were separated."

His blush was endearing. "Can you blame me? All of you are so stupid tall compared to me, so I had to even the playing field a little. The extra inches down there were a nice bonus."

I chuckled at how very him that reaction was. "I'm certainly not complaining or judging." Alistair's naked body touching mine while his erection pressed insistently against me drove me wild. It was utter madness, and I couldn't get enough as I rutted against him.

He may not have been my mate, but I wanted to take my time to explore Alistair and treat him with tenderness. My beast had no patience for that, pushing me to be more aggressive and dominant. I compromised by taking our arousals in hand, slicking them with my magic, which allowed me to pump them both as we frotted. His nails dug into my shoulder while his other hand threaded through my hair, tugging on it in a way that drove me and my beast wild.

Want, need, claim, mine, echoed within me as the pleasure spiraled higher. But I had enough of my mind left to know that Alistair was not mine to claim. As much as I wanted to take him, I refused to go that far. Instead, I continued jerking us both off while kissing him with ardent passion.

When he came all over my fist, the scent of his seed almost snapped my self-control. I burned from how badly I needed him, experiencing an unbearable urge to mount him, to fill him with my cum and mark him as *mine*. Why was I reacting like he was my mate when he wasn't?

Licking his release off my hand triggered my orgasm, with me and my beast deriving intense satisfaction from seeing the evidence of our pleasure decorating his skin.

I couldn't find the words, so I settled for kissing Alistair again, this time with a tenderness that moved something deep within my heart. It was a dangerous game to play with my desire, but damned if he wasn't the most tempting thing in all of Wonderland.

Well, I hadn't gotten fucked, but indulging in the hottest mutual masturbation ever was a nice consolation prize. I stared up at Bianco with awe. "That was *amazing*."

"You are far too tempting," he murmured, leaning in to give me another kiss that caused my heart to flutter from its tenderness. "I need to be careful around you."

"I'd rather you get into trouble with me instead." While I never would have been so daring in my real life, when I was in Wonderland, why couldn't I be anyone I wanted? If anything, I owed it to myself to be so suave and charming. "Especially the sexy kind of trouble. Repeatedly. And as often as possible."

His unrestrained laugh was beautiful to me. "Alas, I have other duties to attend to tonight. In the meantime, you should rest." He gave me a kiss before he sat up, then used his magic to clean us both up and put our clothes back on.

It was badass as hell, but I couldn't help but pout at the signal that it was an end to sexy times for the night. "You're really going to leave?"

"Only for fear that if I don't, I'll never go." God, how did he say the swooniest shit without it being smarmy as fuck? "I'll return in the morning, though."

With a final kiss, Bianco left me alone. I was dazed with satisfaction, despite still technically being a virgin. But frotting and getting a blow job from the hottest guy in two worlds in a single day, after a lifetime of celibacy, was a good enough start to my journey in Wonderland. I didn't have to tick every box off my virgin checklist on the same day. At least it gave me more to look forward to tomorrow.

Pushing those thoughts aside, I entered the most luxurious bathroom I had ever seen. There wasn't a shower but an enormous red tub with golden Jabberwocky feet as the centerpiece of the massive space. I approached it, but there weren't knobs to turn on the water or a spout for it to come out of like I expected. Since I couldn't figure out how to work it, I was about to give up for the night before I remembered I had assistance.

"Twinkle, would you mind filling the bath for me?" I asked the surrounding silence.

A golden Jabberwocky head faucet appeared,

pouring out steaming hot water into the tub. As it began to fill quickly, I searched for a towel but to no avail. "Sorry, may I please have a towel, Twinkle?"

The fluffiest red towel I had ever seen appeared next to the tub in response.

"Thanks, Twinkle." Because of the presence of magic, I felt self-conscious about stripping naked. I waited until the water turned off and the Jabberwocky head disappeared before I took off my clothes and got into the steaming hot water.

It was big enough for me to stretch out as I made myself comfortable. The water was rose scented and helped me relax further. I closed my eyes and focused on trying to find the magic within me that Bianco swore was there. Try as I might, I couldn't sense anything magical. I was just a normal guy, with nothing remark-able about him. What made him think I was special?

The depressing thought made me sink into the water with a heavy sigh. Maybe I should slow things down. What if Bianco freed my magic quickly and then sent me home since he'd have no further use of me? That would be the worst fate ever to learn of such an amazing place as Wonderland and not be allowed to stay.

If I didn't know any better, I swore there was a comforting brush of my hair to soothe my fears. Was that Twinkle or my imagination? It was hard to tell in Wonderland.

"Twinkle, do you think I'm the real Alice?" Silence answered me, so I tried a different tactic. "Could you give me a sign if you do?"

In answer to my question, a sudden heat flared on my right ring finger. I opened my eyes and brought my hand out of the water in time to watch a metal band forming. It was expanded into the shape of a white rabbit's profile, made of glittering enamel with a sparkling pink diamond heart for an eye. The stunning piece of jewelry reminded me that Alice came to Wonderland by following the White Rabbit to the Kingdom of Hearts the same way I did. Maybe it was foolish to think that was proof that I was the proper heir of Alice, but it comforted me all the same.

I brushed my finger over the exquisite craftsmanship, touched by the gift. "Thank you, Twinkle. It's beautiful."

In response, shampoo appeared in my hair, worked by magical means as it lathered up without my help. It was like the best massage in the world, so I soaked up the care. I loved the experience until Twinkle dunked me without warning to rinse off the suds.

I came up spluttering with a laugh as I wiped the water from my eyes. "A little notice would be nice, Twinkle."

The next time he rinsed my hair, it was at a much slower rate, giving me a second to take a breath first. It was an odd experience being bathed by magic, but I found it delightful to have something taking care of me after being alone for so many years.

When Twinkle deemed me finished, the water drained out of the tub. I grabbed the towel before standing up to dry off, then wrapped it around my waist. A puff of warm air dried my hair while invisible fingers straightened it into place.

A toothbrush and toothpaste waited for me at the sink. It tasted like a wild berry I couldn't identify as I brushed my teeth. After finishing, I returned to the bedroom, where the red silk pajamas were spread out for me. I changed into them before getting into bed with a contented sigh.

When I tried to take the ring off, it refused to budge. "Am I supposed to always leave this on?" I asked.

A reassuring pat on the head and a gentle squeeze of my hand with the ring on it answered my question.

I wasn't sure what Twinkle's reasoning was, but there had to be some kind of logic to it. "Okay. I won't try to take it off again." I settled down on the bed, and the lights turned off, surrounding me with darkness. "Thanks, Twinkle. Goodnight."

I could have sworn the magic gave me a good-night kiss on my cheek. It made me smile as I snuggled into the sheets.

Before falling asleep, I said a silent prayer that I'd wake up in Wonderland in the morning and not back in my apartment. More than anything, I wanted my amazing day to be more than a wonderful dream. I needed it to be *real*.

The sound of knocking woke me up. I squinted against the bright sunny day, needing a moment to process that I wasn't back in my shitty apartment but in my grand suite in the Palace of Hearts. A bubble of joy overtook me as I rejoiced that yesterday really happened.

"Alistair, are you awake?" Bianco called out to me from the other side of the door.

"Yes!" Normally, I wasn't much of a morning person, but I was in an extraordinarily good mood from discovering I was still in Wonderland.

"Twinkle, please help Alistair get dressed for breakfast with King Rei," Bianco requested.

I blanched a little at the information. The king hadn't been my biggest fan yesterday. "I'm dining with him?"

"Yes, and I'll be joining you."

That made me feel a little better. Maybe it wouldn't be so awkward with Bianco there. "Okay, I'll be right out."

I hurried through getting ready, although I couldn't help but be a bit miffed Bianco hadn't wanted to enjoy a morning romp with me. I put on the clothes Twinkle laid out for me on the bed while I had used the bathroom. It was an exquisite red tunic with gold filigree hearts on it and a comfortable pair of white britches that tucked into my maroon-and-gold leather boots. I was way overdressed for breakfast, but then again, I was dining with a king. Despite my concerns, I felt like a million bucks when I walked out of my room to meet Bianco.

But I didn't look anywhere near as amazing as him. He was breathtakingly beautiful in a pink three-piece suit with gold accenting on his vest and tie. It brought out the color of his unusual eyes, which caused my heart to skip a beat.

I reflexively touched the white rabbit ring on my hand. It was weird to be so shy in front of him after everything we had done the day before. "Good morning."

He gave me a kind smile. "You look resplendent this morning, Alistair. Come, let's go meet with the king."

I followed him out of my room and fell into step beside him as he led us through the winding hallways and corridors of the palace. "So, is this a onetime thing, or will we do this every morning?"

"I'm not sure. I guess we'll see how today goes."

His answer didn't make me very hopeful. "Should I be worried?"

"No, today should go much better with only the

three of us present. I'd advise you not to mention your other acquaintance to keep the peace, though."

It didn't escape my attention that Bianco didn't use Cheshire's name. "Does using you-know-who's name really summon him?"

Bianco chuckled as we turned another corner. "Not always, but it happens with enough frequency to make it prudent not to use it in the king's presence."

"I'll be careful, then." And I silently warned myself to be on my best behavior and try not to be too crude in front of royalty.

I was hopelessly lost by the time we reached King Rei's personal quarters and were shown to his private dining room. While I had expected an enormously long table that would require us to shout to have a conversation like in the movies, it was a sensible size that made for an intimate setting.

We bowed to the king, who tilted his head in acknowledgment. It surprised me he wasn't wearing his crown and wore a simple red silk tunic and plain black britches. Without all the finery and regalia, King Rei wasn't nearly as intimidating to me as he had been yesterday, although he still had an air of weariness about him that made my heart ache for him.

He gave a small smile. "Please, join me."

Bianco directed me to sit at the other head of the table while he took a seat on the side. I sat on the gold chair that looked more like a throne, with its red velvet cushioning on the seat and back. It was surprisingly comfortable for something that looked so stiff and formal.

Once we were settled, a servant in a red tux served tea. King Rei waited until he finished to ask me, "How was your first day in Wonderland, Alistair?" It was a relief that he didn't call me Alice.

I tried not to gush too much. "It was amazing, Your Majesty. I've never been so well taken care of in my entire life. That was the best night of sleep I think I've ever had." I left out the part where it was because Bianco had given me such a satisfying orgasm right before bed.

The pleased smile he gave me took years off his face. "I'm glad to hear it. As Wonderland is your new home, it's important for you to be at ease here. I apologize for not giving you a warmer welcome yesterday."

I couldn't wrap my head around the fact that a *king* was apologizing to *me*. "It's okay! I don't blame you for not being impressed with me. I'm not very impressed with myself most of the time, either."

"There is nobody I trust more in this kingdom than Bianco. If he chose you and Vivalter agreed, then you're our one and only Alice." He took a sip of tea, making the simple action look incredibly elegant and refined. "You have come a long way to help. We owe you a debt of gratitude. If there is anything we can do to make your time here more comfortable, all you must do is ask."

"Oh, I couldn't possibly ask for more!" The thought boggled my mind. "You've already been so generous. Anything else would be the height of greediness."

His unusual red eyes studied me with interest as I drank my delicious tea. "You're more modest than I would have expected."

"The original Alice never liked to trouble anyone, either. In that, they are the same," Bianco said. "Although I must admit, I'm curious where you got that." He pointed at my hand holding my delicate, heart-shaped teacup.

I touched the ring as my stomach churned with nervousness. "Twinkle gave it to me last night and told me not to take it off."

One of the king's auburn eyebrows arched upward. "Twinkle? There's a name I haven't heard of in a *very* long time."

"It seems Twinkle found a relic I gave Alice all those years ago." Bianco surprised me by reaching out to take my hand in his, running his thumb over the jewelry. It made my breathing hitch in surprise, almost as if my fiancé were inspecting the engagement ring he gave me. Why did that thought make me feel like a giddy school-girl with her first crush? "I gave her this as a way of summoning me, no matter where she was in our world. All she needed to do was wish for me to join her wherever she was so I could help her with anything."

"Does that still work?" I asked. It seemed like it

could come in handy if we were ever separated and I found myself in trouble.

"The magic is active, so in theory, it should work the same way. But I'm not sure if it would be possible for it to work over such long distances with that weak state of magic in Wonderland now."

The king's eyes narrowed with displeasure. "Even when they are an ally, they continue to be a problem to this day."

Bianco let go of my hand, making it a little easier for me to breathe. Good humor laced his tone. "You only say that because of the rumors that King Otto of Mirror-land is looking for suitors for his son, Prince Renner, now that he is almost of age."

"Our alliance is not so weak that I would have to marry in order to secure it," King Rei said with a scowl.

"It's not the worst idea in the world." Bianco's response shocked me since I thought he was Team Cheshire for the king's partner. "Plus, Prince Renner has a reputation for being as kind as he is attractive. He would make an excellent consort for you."

The king bristled with irritation. "We're *not* discussing this. I will never agree to such an absurd prospect."

"Would you rather end up with the Princess of Diamonds?" Bianco asked. The king's nose wrinkled with disgust, making Bianco chuckle. I wondered what was so wrong with her. "That's what I thought. Prince

Renner is one of the last eligible royal bachelors left who isn't already betrothed. Your only other alternative is—"

King Rei held up his hand to stop him. "I don't need to hear it."

"Even if I don't say it, we both know what would make you happiest." It didn't take a genius to figure out they were talking about Cheshire. "It would also be your only legitimate reason to turn down a proposal from Prince Renner. Without having a partner, you leave yourself vulnerable to these types of situations."

Before the king could respond, breakfast was served. It appeared to be some pastries, fresh wild berries, and things that looked like sunny-side eggs but had red yolks instead of yellow. There was also some kind of sausages, but they didn't smell like what I was used to. While it was unusual, my stomach rumbled with approval.

"What good is being a king if I can't do what I damn well please?" King Rei groused as he picked up a pastry and started spreading butter on it.

"I believe that is exactly my point." Bianco ate what appeared to be a breakfast salad, which made sense since he was a rabbit shifter. "Being able to do what you want includes being with who you really want to be—"

King Rei leveled a warning glare at Bianco that made him stop speaking. "It's not up for discussion."

"It'll need addressed soon, or Prince Renner will

become your problem. And I think we all know what the consequences of *that* will be when certain parties find out about a potential engagement to another man." Bianco took a bite of a pastry. "I'm merely looking out for your best interests and trying to save you future headaches *and* heartaches."

King Rei sighed with a resigned look. "You're a wonderful friend, Bianco. I'm just so tired of this endless game."

"Luckily for you, it's a very easy one to win—if you're brave enough to make the right move." Bianco sipped his tea, looking at the ruler with a knowing expression over the rim of his cup. "But that's enough of that for now."

My breakfast was as incredible as dinner had been the night before, making it hard not to squeal with delight as I thoroughly enjoyed myself, despite the awkward silence that descended upon us as we all ate.

It surprised me when King Rei spoke after a bit. "Do you really think King Otto would try to use Prince Renner to renew our alliance?"

"It would be very smart of him to do that."

King Rei frowned as he finished what looked to be a scone with clotted cream. "Perhaps I would have been better off if my family *had* married me off when I was a child. Then I wouldn't suffer so much."

Bianco snorted in amusement. "If you think that

would have stopped your beloved, you don't know him as well as you think."

The king gave a heavy sigh. "No, you're right. And before I inherited the crown, I would have rebelled and done as I pleased."

"You still can," Bianco urged him. "You've been good enough to your people that they would support you, no matter who you end up with."

"It's a nice thought, but it's not possible." King Rei sighed again before shifting his attention to another topic. "Bianco, what are your plans for Alistair?"

"For today, I was planning on taking him to meet Hatter and see if he had any sage words of wisdom." Bianco's pronouncement excited me, but I tried not to show it. I couldn't believe I was going to visit the famous Mad Hatter! "Vivalter and March will most likely be around for a tea party."

That drew a chuckle from King Rei. "Nobody throws a better tea party than that group. It's been too long since I've been able to partake in one with them."

"I'll try to plan one for everyone later, then."

"Just make sure they know it's by private invitation only and they can't bring *friends*," King Rei said with emphasis, although it was clear he only meant Cheshire. "I won't take kindly to the event being crashed by unwelcome interlopers."

Bianco tilted his head in acknowledgment.

"Respectfully, I don't think they have any more say in the matter than you do."

The corner of the king's mouth turned up in a slight smirk. "That's true."

I was sad when I finished my meal because it was so damn tasty.

Bianco stood up with a bow, gesturing for me to do the same. "We will leave you to the rest of your day, Your Majesty. I'll report back if I hear anything of interest."

"Thank you for a truly wonderful breakfast, Your Majesty," I added. Despite some of the awkwardness, I had mostly enjoyed myself.

"You're very welcome." King Rei gave me a genuine smile. "Please give my regards to Hatter. If Vivalter is there, tell him I'll have need for him soon."

Bianco gave a formal bow. "I will do so."

After a few more parting words, we left to start on our next adventure of meeting the famous Mad Hatter I had always been such a fan of in the original stories.

After breakfast, Alistair and I began the walk to Hatter's house. Since it was a pleasant day, I opted to stay in my human form as we made the journey.

"Can I ask a question?" Alistair worried his lower lip, as if he feared I would reject his request.

"Of course."

"So, Vivalter is, uh, you-know-who's brother, right?"

I chuckled at his caution in not summoning Cheshire so close to the palace. "Indeed. They are a curious pair of siblings."

"If they're related, why would the king want to meet with him? When he has issues with one brother, wouldn't the other be a problem?"

I was silent for a moment as I figured out how to best answer his inquiry. "Before he is a brother, Vivalter is the king's royal seer first. Their personal lives are secondary to their official roles."

"Royal seer?" Alistair glanced up at me with a puzzled expression. "What's that?"

"Vivalter foretells the prophecies of what is yet to come. It is with his help that I could find you. He's also the one who pronounced that you must forge a loving bond to save Wonderland." I still appreciated the guidance Vivalter had provided me to find our long-lost Alice. "He is a wise soul, but sometimes he speaks in complicated riddles that can be confusing. It's one of the few traits he and his brother share."

"That's so cool," Alistair said in an awed voice.

"He smokes certain herbs to help him look into the future, which you undoubtedly noticed yesterday." It was hard not to when the fragrant smoke always followed him. "You most likely felt a bit dazed around him, but that's a side effect of the herbs."

"It was almost like a contact high. But I wasn't sure if it was the smoke or the fact he's ridiculously attractive." Alistair's cheeks turned a becoming shade of pink. "Everyone in Wonderland is. I'm so plain next to all of you."

"Not at all. You're incredibly handsome in your own right." I glanced over at him, finding him staring at me in disbelief. "Surely, that doesn't come as a surprise to you?"

He brushed his fingers against his cheek to see if

they were flushed. "At best, I'm that semi-cute, awkward boy next door, but everyone here is god-tier gorgeous. I can't compete."

"It appears we need to work on your self-esteem while you're here." I mentally added it to my to-do list. It simply wouldn't do to have a self-conscious Alice.

He snorted in amusement. "Good luck. I have a lifetime of people telling me I'm not good enough."

"Then it appears the Overlanders are the maddest of us all." I shook my head in amazement that anyone could overlook a star shining as brightly as Alistair. "It would be an honor to be with someone as remarkable as you."

"Now you really are making me blush." The color reached to the tips of his ears. "But I don't get it. I tried to find the magic within me last night, but there's nothing there. I feel like the same normal guy as always. It makes me afraid there must be some mistake because there's no way someone as ordinary as me could be Alice."

"Without a doubt, you are our Alice. Across all the people in time and space, only your magic has tugged on my soul and brought me to find you." It was a most curious experience. "I can feel the rightness of it to the core of my being. But if it would reassure you, I can show you where the magic lies within you once we are at the palace later."

"It would help. I hate feeling like I'm wasting your

time when you have been so kind and generous to me." His bashful smile was endearing. "I really want to be your Alice so I can stay here."

That surprised me. "You don't wish to return home?"

"Like I said before, there is no home to go back to. It might be nice to pick up a few things, but if it meant risking not being able to come back to Wonderland, it's not worth it to me."

"Once you've formed a bonding love with Wonderland, it should anchor you here and allow you free passage between our realms. There's even a chance that you'll be powerful enough to imagine what you want from your home, then have it appear here to save you the trip." Alice had been able to do it, so I was confident the same would be true of Alistair. "It'll be easier once the magic has been restored to our lands."

"That would be amazing if I could do that before my rent is due next month. I have a few things I'd love to save before my landlord trashes it all." There was an extra bounce in his step as we neared the entrance to the woods. "Can I ask another question?"

It was cute how eager he was to learn more. "Sure."

"You mentioned Prince Renner of Mirrorland earlier. Is that the same place as Looking-Glass Land from the books?"

"During the Magic Wars, Looking-Glass Land broke into two factions. The Mirrorland reformers wanted to remake the country into something more progressive. They felt Looking-Glass Land was too stuck in their old ways. In the end, we're all fortunate that the Mirrorland faction won their internal civil war. King Otto and Queen Emme have been very good to their people, and Prince Renner is a wonderfully compassionate heir. The spoiled Princess of Diamonds could learn some things from him about empathy and compassion."

"I was surprised that you seemed to support King Rei being with Prince Renner, considering how supportive you were of him being with his actual partner." Alistair ran his fingers through his hair with a concerned expression. "I'm sorry if that's out of line to say."

His confusion was understandable. "Truthfully, Prince Renner *would* make a wonderful consort for King Rei, if it weren't for the added complication of who he should be with instead." As long as Cheshire lived, he'd never allow his fated mate to be with anyone else, though. "But I've heard rumblings of rumors that Prince Renner might travel soon to meet other prospective royals about the possibility of an engagement before his coming-of-age ceremony. When King Rei is unattached in the public eye, it is an open invitation to Prince Renner to court him."

"But if he did, wouldn't it cause enormous problems between King Rei and—" Alistair cut himself off as he tried to find another word to use in place of Cheshire's name. "Well, I can't imagine *he* would take too kindly to that kind of interference."

Cheshire would never stop until King Rei was his again. "Perhaps it makes me a terrible friend, but I'm hoping that it will force King Rei to choose happiness once and for all."

"What happens to Prince Renner if King Rei doesn't choose him?" Alistair asked.

"Hopefully, he will find someone else capable of loving him the way he deserves."

Alistair heaved a sympathetic sigh. "Poor King Rei. I hope he can choose love before it's too late."

"I'm sure he will." It was only a matter of time before Cheshire persuaded his stubborn mate to give in to him. And I'd certainly do everything in my power to help my two dear friends find the love together that they deserved.

My answer seemed to satisfy Alistair. "What about Hatter? Does he actually sell hats, or does he do something else?"

"Oh, he does much more than hats. He's Wonderland's premier fashion designer. We're his biggest client since he provides all the clothing for the royal House of Hearts. We have the best-dressed court in all the lands because of him." I gestured at our outfits. "We're both wearing his designs right now."

Alistair smoothed the front of his tunic. "That's a relief. I would have felt awful showing up at Hatter's doorstep in another designer's clothing. Talk about awkward!"

His adorable reaction amused me. "Owing to his friendship with the king, Hatter is never too busy to provide us with the finest outfits Wonderland offers. We are truly fortunate that King Rei didn't share the same distaste for Hatter as the former Queen of Hearts."

He hummed with interest. "Is there anything I should know before I meet him?"

While I didn't want to ruin the fun surprise about Hatter's appearance, it was only fair to give him some background. "The March Hare from the books works for him as a right-hand man, so March is almost always with Hatter, unless he's away on an errand for business."

"What about the Dormouse who always slept?"

"He's a shifter who is trapped in his animal form," I explained. "He didn't have much contact with the original Alice because he was hibernating, so he didn't have enough magic remaining to shift into his human form after she left Wonderland."

Alistair seemed surprised. "Wait, so there are other shifters who are stuck in their animal form and can't turn back into humans?"

"Yes, and there are shifters who are in their human form who can no longer shift into their animal one because of the lack of magic. The only ones who can still freely shift between forms are Cheshire, Vivalter,

March, and myself." I chuckled when I noticed Alistair glancing around us for the mercurial cat since I had mentioned his name. "This is a conversation that wouldn't interest him, so he won't appear. However, it would be very Cheshirelike to show up simply because I said he wouldn't."

Alistair laughed. "True."

"It wouldn't surprise me if he appears at the tea party. Vivalter is almost certainly going to be there."

"Why would he be there?"

"He's *very* close to Hatter," I said, although there was a great deal more to their situation than that. "Wherever Hatter is, Vivalter is never far."

"Is it because they're best friends or something more?"

I ruefully shook my head. "That is a question for the ages."

Alistair's expression reflected his confusion. "What do you mean?"

"The only people who don't know Hatter and Vivalter are in love with each other are them." As someone who had watched them dance around each other for centuries, it was equal parts amazing and frustrating. "Whether it's willful ignorance or utter oblivion is up for debate."

Alistair's eyebrows arched up in surprise. "Really?"

"There's no reason for them not to be together, so it's a genuine mystery why they continue to only be 'dear friends,' as they call themselves." It was confounding when they weren't hampered by positions like King Rei and Cheshire were. "I learned to stay out of it long ago. Cheshire is the only one who hasn't grasped that lesson. Like the baby brother he is, there are few things he enjoys more than meddling with those two."

"Don't they get mad at him for doing that?" Alistair asked.

"Hatter simply laughs it off. Vivalter puts up with it to a point, but he usually ends the game by reminding Cheshire of his own romantic situation." It was a scene I had watched play out so many times over the centuries that I sometimes wondered if it was a consequence of the endless tea party time loop the former Queen of Hearts had trapped Hatter within for years. "If it happens today, I recommend staying out of the fray and letting the brothers play their game as they please."

Alistair tapped his chin thoughtfully as we continued walking. "Speaking of brothers, what about Tweedledee and Tweedledum? Are they still around?"

The names took me back to when Alice first appeared in our world. "At some point, they renounced their Looking-Glass Land heritage and worked as royal guards at the Palace of Mirrors, but it has been quite some time since I heard about that unruly duo. They may have moved on since then."

"I can only imagine how much more argumentative

they are now that they're older." Alistair wrinkled his nose in distaste.

"Thankfully, Hatter and his crew are more pleasant to associate with," I said. "It's not that much farther."

The way Alistair lit up with joy was precious. Why couldn't I stop noticing he was too cute for words?

CHAPTER
ELEVEN

ALISTAIR

Based on the books, I had expected Hatter to have a small house with a thatched roof somewhere deep in the forest. Nothing prepared me for the sprawling palatial residence we arrived at after our pleasant walk through the woods. The mansion was practically a castle, complete with top hat turrets and heart-shaped windows.

My stupid mouth reacted before my brain could stop it. "Wait, Hatter lives *here*?"

Bianco chuckled at my reaction but not unkindly. "Yes, when he's not traveling for fittings for his prestigious clients like King Rei."

Given how generous the ruler had been to me and how luxurious everything surrounding him was, it made sense that he paid Hatter well enough to live like the king he dressed. But it was still a shocking display of wealth that left me in awe as Bianco led me up the long stone driveway. I wondered if there would be any suspiciously naked cherubs on Hatter's ceiling?

The narrow road expanded into an expansive courtyard that was full of greenery and roses of every color imaginable. In the center was an enormous fountain that featured a giant butterfly standing on an amethyst top hat. The glittering gems decorating it were dazzling in the dappled sunlight filtering through the trees. Its beautiful wings flapped, sending spray cascading everywhere in a stunning water show that left me captivated.

It was such an impressive display that it took a few moments for it to register the significance of having a butterfly standing on a hat sculpture fountain. "Wait, is this supposed to be Vivalter and Hatter?"

"Indeed. He commissioned it as an artistic celebration of their friendship." The corner of Bianco's mouth turned up as he studied the fountain. "He claims not to understand why anyone would consider this a romantic declaration."

"The butterfly is so beautiful. How could it not be?" It was the most amazing fountain I had seen before. Those two *had* to be fucking, right?

"Welcome to the mad world of Hatter."

A servant greeted us at the door with a low bow as we approached. The man was the first genuinely aged person I had seen since I had arrived, making me wonder how old he was. He was short in stature, with gray hair and a kindly face. His stylish teal uniform, trimmed with gold embroidery, was tailored to perfection. "Welcome, Honorable Bianco and guest."

"I hope you've been well, Pellagrio," Bianco said with a friendly smile. He gestured at me. "This is Alistair Hargreaves."

"It's nice to meet you, Pellagrio." I wasn't sure if I was supposed to offer to shake his hand, since Bianco hadn't prepped me on the rules of dealing with servants in Wonderland outside of the king's palace. It was easier to wait for his reaction and go from there.

He stared at me with wide brown eyes. "You are very kind to say so, sir. Please follow me."

We followed Pellagrio through the immaculately decorated home that rivaled the Palace of Hearts for its luxurious grandeur. It was giving me cognitive dissonance compared to how different the reality was from the simple illustrations about Hatter's tea party. But on the upside, at least there wasn't a naked baby cherub with his dick out anywhere in sight.

The servant led us to an outside terrace, which took my breath away. Lush forest greenery stretched as far as the eye could see, but the centerpiece was the massive waterfall over a stone cliff that poured into a lake with the bluest water I had ever seen. It was breathtakingly beautiful. I could barely take my eyes off it to focus on the person who stood up as Pellagrio announced our presence.

The mismatch between the book and reality about Hatter's home was nothing compared to the man himself. Instead of a short, wizened old man who had lost a battle with Father Time and was trapped in an endless tea party, he was another impossibly beautiful person who looked to be in his thirties.

Despite my newly gained inches, he was still taller than me, with a lean figure that was made even more impressive by the impeccably tailored outfit he wore. It reminded me of a royal purple-and-silver wizard robe, with kimono-style folds over his chest that were under the jacket and long sleeves that were split to show the complicated embroidery on his arms. The panel in front of his legs had similar silver detailing on the bottom and added to the illusion that he was over seven feet tall.

Hatter had wavy blue hair that framed his face in the front. His turquoise eyes studied me with interest. There was something timeless about his youthfulness, with high cheekbones and a sharp jawline that almost made him too pretty to look at directly. What the fuck was in the water in Wonderland to make everyone so gorgeous?

"Well, well, well," he said in a baritone voice that sent shivers racing down my spine. He took a step closer to me, making my stomach do an entire gymnastics routine. His pleased smile was dazzling. "Our long-lost Alice has finally come home at last."

I didn't know what to say, but it didn't seem to

bother him as he embraced me tightly. A faint whiff of the same heady herbs that Vivalter had been smoking made me dizzy. It sent me reeling when my head was already spinning from how radically different the man standing before me was to my pop culture expectations of a frazzled hair weirdo.

When he pulled back, he clasped my shoulders and gave them a firm squeeze as he smiled down at me with a fondness I didn't understand. "Welcome back to Wonderland. I almost didn't believe Vivi when he told me you had returned. But it really is you." He went over to hug Bianco as I tried to gather my bearings and process that he called Vivalter by a name as cute as "Vivi" when the man was sexy as fuck. "Well done, my friend. Congratulations on doing what no one else could."

"Perhaps you should save the congratulations until I've freed his magic," Bianco said with a laugh.

"Nonsense. This is an occasion worthy of a celebratory tea party. Come, join me." He brought us over to a long table under a pergola that was covered in ivy and exotic flowers. "Pellagrio, please prepare a tea party worthy of our dear Alice's return."

The servant bowed low before he hurried off to take care of the request.

Hatter took a seat at the head of the table, then gestured for me to sit on the side next to him. He was so regal in his bearing that I almost felt like I should bow to him, but I refrained from acting on the impulse. Bianco sat beside me, which calmed my nerves. Although, a little warning about gauging my expectations would have been nice so I wasn't blindsided by Hatter being so different from the pictures and movies I had seen.

"I must say, it is quite unexpected that you are a he and not a she," he commented as he continued looking me over with his turquoise eyes that seemed to glow with an unnatural light. "What a delightful surprise."

Before I could reply, someone approached us. It was another absurdly handsome man, who had luscious brown hair with a gentle wave in it that beckoned you to run your fingers through it. He wore a black tunic with an intricate brocade trimmed with red metallic threading and a high collar. It was paired with plain black britches, giving him the look of a lethal assassin from a badass action movie. I sat up a little straighter in my chair when his gaze met mine.

"Ah, excellent timing as always, March," Hatter greeted him. "Meet our new Alice."

It surprised me when March sat in the seat across from Bianco, leaving the one next to Hatter and opposite me empty. He gave me a look over that made me feel shy to have so much undivided attention from so many ridiculously attractive people. It was also giving me a complex about how many famous characters from a children's book I would have been willing to let rail me. "Funny, I thought Vivalter was joking when he said we had a male Alice. Interesting."

I awkwardly waved at him. "Hi."

"You're as cute as he promised." His lips quirked up in a smirk. "Speaking of which, where is Vivalter?"

"Oh, you know him. He's always fashionably late," Hatter replied. "As he says, he'll arrive whenever it's time for him to be here."

After my encounter with the nonsensical butterfly shifter, that certainly sounded like some bullshit riddle he'd say. He had thrown me for a loop, and I wasn't sure I could blame all of it on whatever he had been smoking.

"Speak of the devil, and the Dëvîlskātž appears," Bianco said, drawing my attention to a large butterfly flying our way.

Every flap of its wings caused the rainbow markings to sparkle in the sunlight. It was far more beautiful than any butterfly in my world, real or fake.

Hatter held out his outstretched palm, allowing the butterfly to come to a graceful landing on it. "Ah, my dear Vivi, you are as splendiferous as always," he said with genuine awe in his voice.

The creature shifted into Vivalter, although he once again kept his rainbow wings while in his human form. He straddled Hatter's lap while holding his hand in a shockingly intimate position. I couldn't see Vivalter's face, but Hatter appeared to be absolutely delighted to have his best friend in his lap.

"Truly, there is no creature in Wonderland more fantabulous than you, my wondrous Vivi." Hatter looked up at his friend with all the affection in the world, bringing Vivalter's hand up to his lips to kiss before letting go to embrace him.

Vivalter's butterfly wings fluttered slightly, making me aware of the smoky incense smell that tantalized my senses and left me a little heady and aroused, if I was being honest. Or maybe that was just from being around so many fuckable people. "And yet there is nobody as frabjous as you, my dearest friend."

"We make quite the pair, you and I."

"Me and you make far more than that," Vivalter murmured as he leaned forward enough to make me wonder if they would actually kiss.

I held my breath as I waited for it to happen. It was stunning how drastically Bianco had undersold the closeness of the two friends. Anyone looking at the duo would assume they were a couple deeply in love. You could cut the sexual tension between them with a knife —although being in Wonderland, it was probably more appropriate to say a vorpal sword would do the trick instead.

March cleared his throat loud enough to get their attention. "Are you two going to continue basking in your closeness, or can we have some tea?" His euphemism for their intense chemistry made me want to laugh, but I didn't dare under the circumstances.

"Perhaps if you were to find someone yourself, you would not begrudge us so," Hatter said. "You've been alone far too long."

March arched an eyebrow at him. "Working for you leaves me with little time for such dalliances."

"Perhaps I will have to make time for you to indulge in the future."

The hare shifter snorted in a very undignified manner. "Unless I'm entertaining myself with our clients, I don't foresee that happening."

"You're far too serious for someone who lives in Wonderland. You owe it to yourself to have more fun."

"You have plenty of fun for the both of us," March said, his voice full of fondness rather than frustration. "I'm satisfied with my work. That's enough for me until I'm lucky enough to meet my fated mate someday."

"That day will come sooner than you expect," Vivalter said.

March blinked at him in surprise. "You've had visions about it?"

"A fun adventure awaits you amongst the chaos your union will cause."

"Since when am I the one who brings the havoc? That's Cheshire's special brand of mischief."

Vivalter chuckled. "And yet, you will find that you

are just as skilled at unleashing mayhem upon an unsuspecting kingdom."

March could only shake his head in amazement. "Well, as long as we're in love, I suppose it might be worth the consequences."

"It will be," Vivalter predicted with complete confidence.

When Pellagrio appeared with several other servants to serve the tea and treats, Vivalter sighed dramatically as he slid off Hatter's lap to take a seat in the chair by his side. The way he sulked made it very easy to see the relation between him and Cheshire, who was equally dramatic and pouty when he didn't get what he wanted. It made sense now why March had left the chair open earlier. I could only imagine how many times he had sat through similar greetings in the past.

When I glanced over at Bianco, he had a knowing grin on his face. We were definitely going to talk later because there seemed to be a lot more to the story of Hatter and Vivalter than he had originally implied.

A servant set a teacup in front of me, which was as beautifully ornate as Hatter's outfit. I was worried about holding something that looked so expensive for fear that I would chip or shatter it with my natural clumsiness. But I tried to act normal for the sake of not embarrassing myself. Plus, the tea was just as amazing as what they had served at the Palace of Hearts.

"I'm impressed you've already made progress, Bianco," Vivalter said in an airy voice.

"Progress on what?" Bianco asked.

Vivalter's gaze shifted over to me, then back to the White Rabbit shifter. "Staking your claim."

"I don't know what you're referring to." Bianco took a long sip of tea as he stared down Vivalter.

"You've clearly marked your territory." Vivalter's lips curled upward in a knowing smirk that brought a blush to my cheeks. Could everyone smell that we had fooled around with each other? "Or will you deny that?"

"I will deny anything that's not true." Bianco set his teacup down on its plate.

"Anywhere and everywhere, wherever he is." Vivalter's cryptic comment left me more confused than before. "Isn't that right?"

"Is there some reason you're trying to read a deeper meaning into a protective charm?" Bianco asked.

I reflexively touched the white rabbit ring on my right hand. Bianco had said that it potentially had the power to bring him to my side, no matter where he was in the kingdom, provided the magic still worked. Why would Vivalter mention it, though?

"Because there might be a deeper meaning." Vivalter took a sip of his tea. "Or perhaps not. Who knows?"

"I would expect you to know since you're the royal seer." Bianco held Vivalter's gaze. "Do you have anything useful to add, or are you simply enjoying being paradoxical?"

"That remains to be seen."

I warned myself to stay out of it, but my curiosity was too strong. "You told Bianco about the prophecy that I would form a bonding love to save Wonderland, right?"

Vivalter's indigo gaze focused on me. "What of it?"

I doubted I would get a direct answer, but I still had to ask. "Why do you think I have to bond with Wonderland and not a person?"

"I don't think anything." Vivalter shrugged as he tossed some of his rainbow-colored hair over his shoulder. "I only report what I see in my visions."

"And you saw me bonding with Wonderland instead of a person?"

"I have not witnessed the bonding itself. I only know the bond is forged from a great love. It is up to you to define that."

His unhelpful answer caused me to scowl. Why was nothing ever clear with him? I was about to ask a follow-up question when the hairs on the back of my neck stood up. It was an eerie feeling, almost as if someone was watching us. Before my fears could get out of control, something heavy landed on my shoulder. Rather than scaring me, the familiar weight and soft purring told me it was Cheshire.

"Darling brother, you're fooling no one with your

invisibility," Vivalter declared before he took a sip of tea while aiming a piercing look just above me. "It's most unlike you to be so subtle about crashing a tea party."

Cheshire revealed himself in cat form with a haughty sniff. "I'm not crashing anything when I have an outstanding invitation to come and go whenever I please." He jumped off my shoulder and walked over to Hatter and up his arm to his shoulder. To my surprise, he seemed to defy physics by somehow stretching himself around Hatter's neck like a scarf.

Hatter reached up to give the cat a loving scritch behind the ears. "You always have been and will always be welcome here, Cheshire."

Vivalter's jaw muscles tensed at Hatter's open rebellion but said nothing.

"You're so good to me," Cheshire purred as he nuzzled against Hatter. "Does this make you jealous, my beloved brother?"

"I have nothing to be jealous of." Vivalter's irritation told a very different story.

Hatter held Vivalter's gaze. It was like eye-sex at its best. "Yes, because you are my nearest and dearest friend, who I love above all others."

Vivalter looked somewhat appeased by the declaration, but that didn't last long. Not when Cheshire said, "Perhaps if he were your nearest and dearest lover, he would not feel so threatened—"

"Do you not have a king to go bother with your

nonsense?" Vivalter interrupted to ask, a hard edge coming into his voice.

"You call it nonsense, but it makes much sense." Cheshire snickered, causing Vivalter to scowl again. "What kind of seer refuses to see the truth that lies before him?"

"Come now, Cheshire. Do not vex your brother so much," Hatter said, rubbing the cat shifter under the chin. "You know I dislike it when he gets cross with you."

"He is cross with himself, not me." Cheshire slid off Hatter and walked back over to sit in my lap. "Besides, if anyone should be cross, it should be me."

The comment confused me. "Why do you say that?"

"Because it is a heavy burden to be the only one who sees the love that others are quick to deny." Cheshire harrumphed in annoyance. "It grows very tiresome to see those I care about choosing misery over love. I hope you will be different, Alistair. Perhaps it will give others the courage to do the same. Don't you agree, Bianco?"

"Life would indeed be better if everyone could love who they choose," Bianco said in a soft voice that made me wonder if there was somebody he wished he could love and couldn't, even if they weren't a mate. The thought tugged at my heart. It felt a lot like jealousy, but that couldn't be right.

"Be sure to remember that when it matters most." With those words, Cheshire disappeared. He must have left for real because I couldn't feel the weight of him on my lap anymore.

An awkward silence descended over the group. March picked up a teapot and asked, "So, who wants more tea?"

After that, everything went back to normal—well, as normal as anything could be in a place as wonderful and wild as Wonderland. But something told me it wouldn't stay that way for long.

CHAPTER
TWELVE
BIANCO

Before we left, I pulled Vivalter away for a private conversation. "King Rei wanted me to tell you he will summon you to court soon."

"Is it for a particular reason or because he misses me?" Vivalter asked, although I suspected he already knew the answer.

"I believe it is regarding the rumors about Prince Renner, but he didn't share specifics with me."

Vivalter's smile grew into a grin. "Ah, yes. He will certainly make things interesting."

"How so?"

"I have seen enough to know that my brother will have a few surprises in his future because of that handsome complication." Vivalter chuckled with an amused look. "I shall enjoy watching from the sidelines as the situation unfolds."

"Is there anything in particular I need to be prepared for when that time comes?" I asked.

"Wild chaos. But as it usually follows my brother wherever he goes, you should be well versed in handling it by now."

I snorted at the understatement. "Yes, I have plenty of experience with that when it comes to his antics regarding the king."

"There is one thing you should remember, though."

It was unlike Vivalter to volunteer information, so it piqued my curiosity. "What's that?"

"Trust what you feel and ignore what you know. What you have forgotten is the key to everything."

His cryptic message made me want to groan with frustration. It would be nice to have Vivalter skip the riddles at least once in my life. "I don't suppose you're willing to provide me with any specific hints?"

"You will understand when it is time to know."

I held in a sigh at the very Vivalteresque answer. "Do you have any other helpful clues?"

"Remember that we are creatures of instinct. Things may not make sense in our human forms, but they will always be clear when we are one with our beasts." He clasped me on the shoulder and gave it a squeeze. "If you are ever uncertain, remember that above all else."

"Thanks."

When he had nothing further to say, Vivalter and I

rejoined the group long enough to say our goodbyes before I left with Alistair.

He was brimming with excitement. "That was so amazing! I can't believe I met Hatter!" He turned to look at me with a pout. "Why didn't you warn me he looked nothing like the old man in the book?"

"Because I thought it would be more fun for you to be surprised." It had been adorable watching Alistair try to process the fact that Hatter defied time with his youthfulness. "To make it up to you, would you like to ride me back to the palace?"

A faint blush graced his cheeks. "You mean ride you while you're a rabbit?"

"Yes, I'll be big enough for you to ride." It had been a long time since I had been in my rabbit form or carried someone on my back. Vivalter's comment made me curious enough to offer. "We'll return much faster that way."

"Are you sure you won't mind?" He worried his lower lip. "I don't want to disrespect you."

"It's not disrespectful at all." I figured it would be easier to convince him in animal form, so I shifted into a large rabbit. "It's an offer I freely make."

Alistair stared at me with wide eyes full of wonder. "*Wow*, you're so big," he breathed in an awed tone that made me preen. "That's so cool! Am I allowed to touch you?"

"Of course."

He came closer to me, reaching out to pet my side with a murmur of enjoyment. "You're so soft!"

Alistair's scent was pleasing in my human form, but as a rabbit with a more sensitive sense of smell, there was something important I had missed. I had assumed my beast had only been interested in Alistair's magic, but there was a spiced undercurrent to his scent that identified him as our mate. It may have been convinced, but I nuzzled against him under the guise of taking a closer sniff. His pheromones tantalized me, calling out to me to make him mine in a way I was unfamiliar with as he stroked my fur. The more I breathed him in, the more my veins filled with a fiery need that drove me to be bold enough to lick his cheek affectionately because I needed confirmation.

His giggle was adorable, but I was overcome by the taste of him. It was even more enticing than when I had been in my human form. I wanted to pin him down and lick him all over. My beast was in full support of the idea.

Without thought, I rubbed my chin against him, marking him as mine on a primal instinct. It was wildly inappropriate, but it was harder to rein in my animal traits in my rabbit form when my beast was closer to the surface. Vivalter's words from earlier about being one with my beast's senses rang in my mind. Was that what he had been talking about?

"You're certainly affectionate as a rabbit," Alistair

said with a laugh. To my surprise, he nuzzled against my face with his cheek, making the creature inside me ache to claim him as my mate. It was a startling urge. Could he really be my fated mate, and it wasn't just my beast being influenced by Alistair's magic? "Is it bad I enjoy that?"

"Not at all." I couldn't resist rubbing my chin against him again, deriving deep pleasure from marking him as mine as my beast whispered, "Our mate," in my heart. But that couldn't be true, right? "Rabbits enjoy being affectionate. If it was upsetting to you, I would feel terrible about causing you distress."

"I'm more worried about offending you by petting you." He continued stroking my fur before nuzzling against me again with a contented sigh. "You're *so* soft. It makes me never want to stop touching you. But at the same time, I know there's a man in there somewhere, so this is being *super* forward and probably really rude."

I chuckled at his admission, even as I soaked up the affection he was showing me. "Do not feel badly about something I am enjoying immensely."

"But if I stroked your hair this way while you were a human, it would cross a bunch of inappropriate lines."

"Grooming is a way rabbits show closeness to one another, so if you were to stroke or comb my hair in my human form, it would be a very enjoyable experience." The mere thought of it sent a shiver of pleasure through me. "It has been a long time since someone I cared about groomed me."

"You care about me?" Alistair asked in a small voice.

"Of course I do." I nuzzled against him in reassurance. "I have enjoyed getting to know you as Alistair, not Alice."

It amazed me I could smell how happy my comment made him. "For what it's worth, I'm *really* glad I'm your Alice."

"I'm more glad you're my Alistair." The words escaped me without permission as I once again rubbed my chin against him in a subtle claim. I couldn't stop the animal urge to mark him all over, especially when the pleasing scent of his embarrassment tinted with the slightest hint of arousal made my beast go on a rampage like a wild Jabberwocky. The entire world needed to know he was mine.

"Me, too."

If I wasn't careful, my inner creature would say more truths that might get me in trouble. I crouched down lower so he could get into position. "Let's return to the palace."

I appreciated that Alistair was as gentle as possible as he got on top of me.

"Hold on tight," I told him before I began racing back home.

After we had returned to Alistair's room, he seemed a little uncertain. That made two of us since I still didn't know how to handle my beast's conviction that Alistair was our mate. Wasn't it only interested in the magic? Surely, if Alistair was my mate, I would have understood immediately, and it wouldn't have come as such a surprise in my animal form.

Pulling myself from my thoughts, I refocused my attention on him. "What's wrong?" I asked.

"Nothing's wrong, per se. I have a request that's probably a little weird, and I'm not sure if I'm allowed to ask," he said.

I sat beside him on the couch. "You can always ask me anything." The smell of me all over him was quite alluring. And now that I had smelled the pheromones that marked him as my mate in my animal form, it was unmistakable in my human body. How had I missed such a thing? It filled me with most unbecoming urges that were even harder to resist now.

He fidgeted before he glanced over at me. "Could you maybe show me where the magic is inside me? I can't feel anything, and it would reassure me to know it's really there. I'm not sure if that's possible, but…"

"While I'm comfortable showing you where the light magic is, the dark is best left alone until we purify it."

"Does the dark magic live in a certain part of my body? Or is it sort of an all over kind of thing?"

"It is contained to that pit of dread and fear in your stomach. The light magic is different, though. It is suffused throughout you but concentrated primarily on your heart. That's what keeps it so pure." It was a testament to how kind his heart was that it kept the light magic so bright after centuries.

"That's so fascinating!" It was a relief my answer seemed to put him at ease.

"Here, lie down and make yourself comfortable." I stood up so he could stretch out on the couch before I sat down at his side once more.

Placing my hand over his stomach, I summoned my magic. The light magic within him was quick to embrace my power, merging with mine intimately, sending shivers racing down my spine. The emptiness that had always been inside me felt full for the first time in my life. It was as if we had become one, making me more convinced than before that he really was my mate. The more I stretched out my senses, the deeper the connection between us became. It felt like I could crawl into his very soul and find my forever home there. The temptation to do that was almost too much.

See? He's our mate, my beast whispered as it reveled in the magic linking us together. *Claim him now!*

Ignoring my beast's urgings, I slid my hand up to Alistair's heart, letting my magic glide against his as I did so. The pleasure I derived from it was so intense my cock stirred to life. I was too lost in the moment to prevent my body from reacting, especially when the softest keen escaped past his full lips that begged me to kiss them.

When I embraced the light magic encased in his heart, it wrenched a sensual moan from him as his back arched off the couch from the pleasure coursing inside him. It drove me to caress his magic with mine, causing an explosion of ecstasy that rippled through our link. The feeling was exquisite beyond compare as I indulged in the unexpectedly erotic sensation that stoked my arousal to full hardness.

"Y-you have to stop," he pleaded.

I blinked as I came back to myself but not letting go of our connection yet. "Am I hurting you?"

With his flushed cheeks and parted lips, Alistair silently begged me to ravish him. No sooner had the thought crossed my mind than he whimpered, making my hard cock throb with need. "Um, no, quite the opposite, actually. It feels too good, so I'm about to bust a nut. I don't want to make things awkward for you, so unless you intend to do something about it, you should stop before I die of humiliation."

"What is there to be embarrassed about when I'm similarly affected?" I once again caressed him through our magical connection, making us both shudder as it echoed from him through me. "It's an enchantingly erotic sensation, don't you think?"

His gasp of pleasure stirred the thing inside of me that had been unsettled since I had first taken my animal form outside of Hatter's. "Right, it feels *so fucking good*, but if you don't stop—" Alistair cut himself off with a frustrated sound. "Seriously, I'm like three seconds away from exploding in my pants."

My beast accepted his challenge. It intensified our connection, allowing me to project fondness and desire to Alistair.

When my feelings reached him, he gasped with a full-body shudder as he came in his pants as he predicted. It triggered my orgasm from the overwhelming intensity of his. Although my senses were dulled in my human form, the smell of his release sent the creature within me into overdrive, thrashing in its cage and begging for a taste of Alistair's pleasure.

"What was that?" Alistair breathlessly asked, staring at me in shock.

"The way I feel about you." It was easier to say that than explain my beast's involvement.

He struggled to find words. "But that felt a lot like love and *definitely* like lust."

I chuckled at his apt summary. "Indeed."

Alistair blinked at me with an adorably stupefied expression. "I've been here *a fucking day*."

"As Vivalter so kindly reminded me, shifters share the instincts of our inner beasts. That part of me has known since the moment your magic first called out to me that you were mine. Regrettably, I didn't understand until I took my animal form earlier."

It was a relief he wasn't upset by the revelation. "Is that why you were so affectionate in your rabbit form?"

"Yes, my inner beast was quite intent on marking you as ours," I sheepishly admitted. "It's normally dormant since rabbits are not unruly by nature, so I was unprepared for its behavior."

His uncertainty crept in through our connection. "So, it's only the animal part of you that wants me?"

"No, it's not just the creature within me that has an interest in you. I want you, too. And it's not because you're Alice or the magic within you. It's because you're you, which is the most appealing thing of all."

It was faint, but I could feel Alistair trying to embrace me through our connection. "I love I can tell that's true because of whatever it is you're doing with magic."

"I am loath to give up this connection when it's such a genuine pleasure to indulge in you," I admitted.

"Will this go away once you release the magic inside me?"

"Truthfully, I'm not sure how much will remain afterward." His expression fell, so I did my best to give him some hope. "However, since Alice herself possessed some magical abilities, I would expect you to keep some level of magic, allowing us to forge this kind of connection." *Especially when we mate*, my beast reminded me.

Happy relief echoed through our connection. "That makes me feel a little better about it, thank you."

Before I could respond, there was a knock at the door. A servant appeared. "King Rei has requested your presence, Honorable Bianco."

"Tell him I will attend to him anon."

The servant bowed in acknowledgment and left, shutting the door behind him.

"Duty calls," I said with a sigh. I gently withdrew my magic from Alistair, but it still disoriented me from losing the connection with him so suddenly.

It pained me when he groaned at the loss. "I never knew it was possible to feel so empty and alone in my own body." Alistair sighed as he sat up to face me. "I enjoyed being able to sense your feelings. We can do that again later, right?"

"Yes, preferably when I'm not on duty to be summoned by the king." I leaned forward and gave him a kiss on the forehead. "I'll be back when I'm done with him. We can talk more then."

Alistair radiated joy. "Okay."

It was almost impossible to pull myself away from

Alistair when I could still smell his lingering arousal and the scent of his seed that drove my inner creature wild. But my sense of duty won out, so I left temptation to go change before my meeting with the king.

THIRTEEN

ALISTAIR

After Bianco left, I lay back down on the couch with a sigh and took a moment to *feel*. The connection we shared through our magic had been the most incredible thing I had ever experienced. I had never felt so loved in my life. The memory of Bianco stroking the magic within me was almost enough to make me hard again.

It was a lot to process that Bianco and his inner beast both were interested in me. I didn't understand what a rabbit would find appealing about me, but there had been no mistaking the intense desire coming from him earlier. Normally, I'd ruin everything by overthinking the situation and telling myself it was all happening too fast. But as incredible as the experience had been, I was ready to ignore my inner cynic and embrace my good luck as part of Wonderland's charm. It was a place where anything could happen, so why couldn't I fall in love with someone as amazing as Bianco so soon?

Rather than think about it, I got up and headed into the bathroom to get clean. It embarrassed me I had come in my pants without being touched. That hadn't happened since I was a horny teenager. But the magical connection between us had been too intense for me to hold back.

Twinkle must have read my mind because a hot bath was already drawn and ready for me. I stripped down and got in the tub, sinking into the steaming water with a sigh. It felt divine. They were spoiling me with living the good life. Every minute I spent there made going back to the real world and all my problems even more unappealing. I was perfectly content to stay in Wonderland forever.

I closed my eyes as I replayed in my mind what had happened on the couch. The memory of his magic sensually caressing me all over made my dick harden. It had been one of the most deeply intimate experiences of my life, almost as if he had been making love to my soul. I ached to experience that again, to be embraced so personally and with so much meaning. And I was dying for him to do that while kissing me at the same time.

The longer I indulged in the memories, the harder it was not to touch my aching arousal. I desperately wanted to jerk off, but I also was *very* conscious of

Twinkle's omniscient presence. While I tried to tough it out, it was too much for me. "Um, Twinkle, please look away," I nervously said. "And forgive me."

I could have sworn I heard faint laughter, but I put it out of my head as I took myself in hand. My ego preened with satisfaction over needing to use longer strokes now that my dick was bigger, thanks to gaining a few extra inches from the Eat Me cake. Wonderland was the *best*.

Since I had the time in the privacy of my bathroom, I indulged myself in the memories of the most gratifying sexual experience of my life while pleasuring myself. But my mind wasn't content to stop at the memories.

Bianco bent down to give me a passionate kiss as he caressed me all over from the inside. I reached up to tug him down closer, running my fingers through his white hair, which was as soft as his bunny fur. He rewarded me by reaching down and wrapping his hand around my hard-on, jerking me off as he continued giving me searing kisses.

"I need you inside me now," I groaned, not content with only being touched.

"Would you appreciate some help?"

I yelped at the sound of Cheshire's voice, opening my eyes to discover him sitting on the rim of the tub with his trademark grin. With a swear, I pulled my knees to my chest to hide my embarrassing situation. "What are you doing in here?"

"Not having as much fun as you." He snickered as I scowled. "The king and Bianco are having a boring meeting, so I came to play with you."

"Next time, please ask before showing up in the bathroom." My cheeks were still flushed from being caught pleasuring myself. "Could you wait outside while I get dressed?"

"Your modesty is so cute," he said in a teasing tone. "Very well. I shall allow it." He disappeared from his face all the way to the tip of his tail.

I hesitated, wondering if he had obeyed my request or only made himself invisible.

"Fear not, dear Alistair. I'm out here," Cheshire called from the bedroom.

I exhaled a sigh of relief. "Twinkle, could you please give me some clean clothes to change into?" At least the sudden shock had caused my arousal to abate.

A pair of white britches and a matching tunic trimmed with gold embroidery appeared beside the tub, along with a towel. I got out and dried off before quickly getting dressed. There was still something embarrassing about being naked in front of Twinkle, even if it was the magic and not an actual person.

When I returned to the bedroom, Cheshire was sprawled out on the bed in his cat form, his striped belly on full display. "Oh, hello there." He curled his feet as he looked at me with wide, guileless eyes to convey his innocence. "I don't suppose you've forgiven me for my surprise visit yet, have you?"

I sat beside him. "It's not that I minded you visiting. It was the 'I was in the bath naked' part that was embarrassing."

"And the 'pleasuring yourself while thinking of Bianco' part, I'd assume?" Cheshire batted his eyes at me, making me simultaneously laugh and want to crawl into a hole and die.

I could deny it, but it was such a relief to have someone to talk to about it that I sucked up my embarrassment. "Can you blame me? He's so thoughtful and kind, not to mention beautiful and magical."

"Would you like to know a secret about him?" Cheshire shimmied on the bed. "I'll tell you for a good belly rub."

"I'll give you one, but you don't need to tell me anything." I indulged Cheshire's wishes, earning loud purrs for my efforts as he luxuriated under the attention.

"Do they have shifters in your world?" Cheshire asked, confusing me with the topic change.

"They only exist in fiction."

He kneaded the air with his paws. "Are you sure about that?"

"Very," I said with a laugh. "Why?"

"Just curious." He hummed with interest. "What do

you know about shifters from the fiction in your world?"

I shrugged. "Not much. I know they're popular in romance novels, but I never read those."

"That's a shame you missed out on that. Shifters are fantastic at romance." Cheshire stretched as I continued rubbing his belly.

"Are you speaking from personal experience?"

"Why yes, *I* am. It's only a certain king who is most unreceptive to romantic attention that's the issue." Cheshire sighed as he rolled onto his side. "If you don't have shifters, does that mean you don't have mates?"

I shrugged. "Some people believe in the idea of a soul mate, who is your one person you're destined to love forever. But reality has taught most of us that soul mates are the dreams of fairy tales."

"Ah, but it is very different in Wonderland. Shifters have fated mates destined to love them, no matter the odds that may stand in their way," Cheshire explained.

It wasn't hard to make the connection. "Like you and King Rei."

He nodded. "Precisely. Stubborn people like him would rebel against that idea, of course. He would resent that the stars foretold who he would love from the very beginning. That's why I've never told him he's my fated mate."

"Do you really think he would reject you because of that?" I asked.

Cheshire rested his chin on his front paws with a glum sigh. "Perhaps. He *is* stubborn like that. But I want him to love me because he wants to, not because he thinks fate brought us together."

I petted Cheshire's head since he seemed so down about it. "Waiting must be so hard for you."

"It's the worst," he said in a rare moment of seriousness. "But I will wait for him forever if that's what it takes."

"For both of your sakes, I hope he doesn't make you wait that long." I offered up a silent prayer that they'd be able to get together sooner rather than later. But his point made me anxious about another issue. "Does Bianco have a fated mate?"

"He does." The two simple words were a crushing blow. "So do Vivalter and March. I've always known that Rei is mine. My dear brother ignores who his is for some inexplicable reason."

Despite the pain in my heart, I was curious. "Is it because it's Hatter or because it's *not* him?"

"See? One day in Wonderland, and you already know Hatter is his fated mate." Cheshire tsked in disapproval. "I have no idea why my older brother insists on feigning ignorance on the matter, especially when his sense of smell is better than mine. Not to mention his reactions to his mate's pheromones."

"You can tell who your mate is by sense of smell?" I asked in surprise.

"Yes, it's unmissable in our animal form. The person smells like yours. It's the most exquisite spice that fills your veins with fire from the very nearness of them." Cheshire sighed. "Unless, of course, your mate ignores your connection. Then you burn for them without the satisfaction of uniting as one."

It was an interesting piece of information I filed in the back of my mind to think about later. "I'm confused. Your brother and Hatter greeted each other very intimately." It was all terribly confusing. "They clearly love each other, so why aren't they together?"

"If you can get a straight answer out of my brother about that—or anything—you truly will be the savior of Wonderland." Cheshire chuckled at his own joke. "Their reasons are their own. I don't pretend to understand them."

"What about March? You said he has a mate, right?" It was easier to ask about him than deal with the pain of knowing there was someone out there for Bianco who wasn't me.

"He hasn't met his yet. Perhaps they have not been born or their paths are destined to cross in the future. While his magic is weak, he's a splendid fellow and very loyal friend and helper to Hatter through it all." Cheshire licked his paw and rubbed it over his ear. "His mate will be lucky once they discover each other."

I couldn't keep the fear out of my voice. "What about Bianco?"

Cheshire got up and sat in my lap, allowing him to nuzzle my chin. "Come now, dear Alistair. Do you think good ol' Cheshire is so cruel as to tell you Bianco belongs to another?"

"No, but I'm scared, anyway."

He rubbed his head against my cheek with a purr. "You have nothing to fear, unless you don't like him."

"Of course I like him." I hugged Cheshire for comfort. Sometimes it was easy to forget there was a man inside of there and he wasn't just a talking cat. "Probably a little too much, if I'm being honest."

"You being honest is the best way to be. And speaking honestly, it has been many centuries since Bianco has had to think about having a mate. Perhaps he has forgotten about it completely." Cheshire stepped out of my lap to sit in front of me, his long tail curled around his feet. "However, I'm quite certain you will be a tempting reminder for him to pay attention to his instincts."

"Do you genuinely think I'm his mate?" The idea of it filled me with a bubble of excitement, despite not knowing the details of what that meant for me.

"My dearest Alistair, ever since our Alice of the past left, Bianco has spent his entire life searching for *you*. It wasn't until your magic called him that he found his reason to be." He gave a dainty sniff. "If that is not the dedicated love of a fated mate, then I must be a mad dog."

"Why are you telling me this?" From what I knew of Cheshire from the books and my short time with him, he was rarely so direct.

"Perhaps it is my selfish hope that if Rei sees you bond with Bianco, he'll realize how much he wants to do that with me. Or maybe I'm being ornery. Who knows?"

"Bond with Bianco? How?"

Cheshire's expression spread into a cheeky grin. "That is a conversation best had with him. I shall bid you adieu and leave you to your fun."

With a final flick of his tail, Cheshire jumped off the bed and was invisible before he hit the floor. I could only blink in astonishment, my head swimming from the revelations that I couldn't wait to talk to Bianco about once he returned later.

O nce I finished filling King Rei in on the uneventful tea party at Hatter's, I headed to my room for a private moment. Between my inner beast's reaction to Alistair in my animal form and the sensual experience of indulging in his magic, I needed some time alone to process everything. It was the only way for me to have answers when I returned to his side later.

I was almost there when I heard an echoing snicker that forced me to hold in a groan. "Don't you have a king to torture, Cheshire?"

The cat shifter's grin appeared first before the rest of his body filled in while he floated near me. "He can wait. You're much more interesting to me right now."

I sighed as I gave in to the inevitable. "And why is that?"

"Because you've had an eventful day."

"And you know this how?" I asked as I resumed walking with him floating alongside me. I could faintly smell Alistair on him, making me suspect the cat had visited him first. My beast stirred with displeasure, but it was hard to be upset when I knew how dedicated Cheshire was to King Rei.

"Call it a cat's intuition."

After reaching my room, I made myself comfortable on the couch and settled against it with a heavy sigh. "Can we please limit the games we play tonight? I'm too tired to be a good sport, old friend."

He sat next to me, studying me with glowing golden eyes. "Why are you so exhausted?"

Rather than get into the details, I settled for the simple answer. "It's been a long day."

"And perhaps you indulged a bit too much in magic, hmm?" He hummed with interest. "It's quite draining when there's so little of it left in this world."

It was definitely part of the reason for my exhaustion. "Very true." I tilted my head to look at him. "But that's not why you followed me here."

"No, I wanted to see if you remembered what you forgot."

"It's bad enough your brother was after me about that. But now you, too?" I ran my fingers through my hair with a heavy sigh. "What are you two so convinced I've forgotten?"

"Something very important when dealing with your Alice-now-Alistair." He stared at me with unblinking eyes. "I thought perhaps you might have remembered after shifting into your animal form earlier today."

Memories of my beast's reaction to Alistair flood me with an uncomfortable heat. "What about it?"

"You didn't notice anything strange?" Cheshire's tail swished behind him.

I gave him an exasperated look. "You know, you could just tell me instead of making me guess based on your vague questions. That would be a lovely change of pace for once."

"But what's the fun in that?" His snickering laugh made me groan. "You must have *some* clue about what I'm talking about."

"None."

"It's the special thing that shifters can do that none of us have done." He scowled as he pinned his ears. "Not for lack of trying on some of our parts, though."

I was confused until his last point. "Claiming our mates?" It was the only thing Cheshire had been unable to do because he had never revealed to King Rei the depth of their connection.

Cheshire's eyes brightened. "Precisely."

"But I don't have a mate." As soon as I said those words, my beast began arguing to the contrary. But I was so used to not having a mate, it was strange thinking of Alistair in that role.

"Incorrect. We all have a mate. March may not have met his yet, but my brother and I both know who our mates are, although we have not been able to claim them because of stupid reasons." Cheshire's tail drooped as he huffed in annoyance. "And then, there's you."

My head hurt from going in circles with his riddles. "What about me?"

Cheshire gave me an unimpressed sniff. "What other reason would you have to possessively mark someone all over with your scent?"

I pressed my lips in a firm line as I struggled to regain control. Finally, I settled for saying, "That wasn't my intention. It just...happened."

"And you haven't asked yourself *why*?" Cheshire tsked in disapproval. "I'm disappointed in you, Bianco. Normally, you are more self-aware than that."

It was hard not to grow defensive. "Look, I haven't exactly had time to figure out my reaction to Alistair in the forest. A lot has happened recently."

"Haven't you learned not to question your beast's instincts?" Cheshire shook his head with a disappointed expression. "There's only one reason it would possessively mark Alistair as yours. Surely, you don't need a bigger clue than *that* to figure everything out."

"My beast is obviously interested in claiming Alistair." Even saying the sentence stirred my soul to clamor to be with him since I wanted him, too. "But what does that have to do with whatever you and Vivalter think I've forgotten?"

"Must I spell *everything* out for you?" Cheshire hung his head with a long-suffering sigh, which was ironic considering what he put me through regularly. "It's a good thing you aren't usually this dense."

Ignoring the jab, I played to his sentimental side. "Can't you help a friend who has done so much for you over the centuries?"

Cheshire walked closer to headbutt my hand for a scritch behind the ears. Despite my annoyance, I indulged him because I could deny him very little. "Fine, I shall ask you the most important question: how do you claim a mate?"

I scoffed. "What do you mean? You mate with them."

He gave me an expectant look. "And that requires you to do what?"

It was such an obvious answer I felt silly saying it out loud. "Make love to your mate."

"I have made love to my mate countless times, but I have not mated him yet. What's the difference?"

That was when it clicked what he was trying to get me to see. It was indeed something that had been so long since it had been relevant that I had completely forgotten about it. "You never formed a mating bond with him."

"And why would that be important for you to remember?"

All the pieces were coming together. "Are you suggesting that the prophecy's loving bond to save Wonderland's magic is Alistair forming a mating bond with me rather than simply loving Wonderland?"

Cheshire crawled into my lap and nuzzled against my chin with a loud purr. "Would that not make more sense, my dear friend?"

I rewarded him with the petting that he was after. "But it's been centuries since a shifter has formed a mating bond with a partner."

"True. But I'm quite confident your beast remembers how, the same as mine." Cheshire purred louder as I continued stroking him. "Your power mixing with Alistair's is the only way to truly purify the dark magic within him and free the light to return to Wonderland."

The thought of claiming Alistair as my mate made my heart sing, telling me Cheshire was most likely correct. I gave him an appreciative kiss on the forehead. "Thank you for helping me see, my dear friend."

"If I may offer one other piece of advice? Since I'm in such a giving mood," he teased.

I rubbed him under the chin and on the cheeks. "I'm listening."

"When you're in your large beast form, it's more in control. If you want to experience your animal instincts while being rational, be a baby bunny." To prove his point, Cheshire shrunk to the size of a kitten. "You can smell the truth and understand it best."

I patted him on the head. "That's very sage advice. If you will excuse me, I believe I need to visit Alistair for an important talk."

"It's just as well. I'm off to go tempt my mate and see if perhaps he's more agreeable to me when I'm in my adorable kitten form." Cheshire jumped off my lap and disappeared.

I lingered for a moment in my thoughts, but he was right. The best place to get answers was with Alistair.

When I entered Alistair's suite, the door to his bedroom was open. I knocked on it, while enjoying the sight of him fresh out of a bath and only wearing a pair of britches. "Sorry that took so long. Do you have a moment?"

"I'm yours for as long as you want." He picked up his shirt, but I was compelled to stop him.

"Actually, would you mind leaving that off?"

His eyebrows arched upward as a faint blush graced his cheeks. "Is there a particular reason?"

"Make yourself comfortable on the bed, and I'll

explain." It pleased me when he obeyed without question, leaning against the propped-up pillows and looking at me with curiosity. "I was wondering if you would be so kind as to indulge me in testing a theory?"

"Of course!" The color in his cheeks deepened. "Especially if it's what you did to me earlier."

I sat down on the bed before I shifted into my animal form that was the size of a baby bunny.

Alistair cooed with delight. "You're so adorable! And so tiny!"

"Would you like to pick me up?" I asked.

He scooped me up with gentle hands as he brought me closer for inspection. "Oh, and your little bunny nose! You're the cutest bunbun I've ever seen!" He bit his lip with a worried expression. "Sorry, that's probably really inappropriate to think when you're also a person, but you're so adorable. I can't help it!"

"I am gratified you find my animal form so pleasing." I stood up on my hind legs, allowing me to nuzzle against his cheek as I once again marked him as mine on instinct. How had I missed that before? It was an unmistakable compulsion to lay claim to him, and it wasn't because of the magic within him.

"You're stunning as a human, too," he admitted with an endearing blush. The smell of his embarrassment was a genuine delight.

I hopped out of his hands onto his chest, moving closer

so I could curl up in the crook of his neck. Taking my time, I breathed him in and focused on my reaction. With more of my rational mind in control, it was easier to recognize that his spiced scent that had been driving me wild in the forest was the call of my mate. It was shameful I hadn't made the connection earlier. But I had been convinced my beast was only interested in claiming Alistair's magic.

When I took another deep breath, his pheromones filled me with a passionate need for Alistair. It was an embarrassment that I had forgotten something so primary to my existence as a shifter. At the same time, I had spent centuries without any trace of a mate. I had given up hope long ago that I would ever find one. But he was right in front of me and more perfect than I could have imagined.

Alistair petted me with a soft touch that brought me immense pleasure. "What theory are you testing?"

"Something I subconsciously noticed in the forest but didn't realize what it was at the time." The longer I breathed him in, the more intoxicating it became. I *needed* my mate. "Something very important."

"What was it?"

Instead of answering, I hopped down to settle over his heart. Once again, his magic reached out to me, but now I recognized it begging me to complete the mating bond to make us whole. It was another subtle detail I had missed before, having been too distracted by the powerful joining of our magic that had been a prelude to the bond we could form if we mated.

It took a moment before I remembered to answer. "The indicators of who you really are to me."

"Your mate?"

I blinked in surprise. "What would you know about that?"

His expression turned sheepish. "It might have come up when I talked to Cheshire earlier tonight."

It seemed my suspicions about my friend paying a visit to Alistair had been correct. I shifted into my human form, pinning him under me in a suggestive position. "And what did you think about that?"

He stared up at me with a look of open desire that made it incredibly difficult not to act on my urges. "That I'd be the luckiest person in Wonderland if that was true."

I traced the outline of his jaw. "Do you understand you'd be bound to me for the rest of our eternal lives?"

"*Our* eternal lives?" His eyebrows furrowed. "How does that work when I'm human?"

"Because your life and soul would be bound to mine when we mate, which means you will share my eternal life span." I rubbed my thumb over his lush lower lip. "It's why a mating bond is so sacred. It binds your hearts and lives together forever."

The corner of his mouth turned up in a smile. "You're trying to warn me about the dangers of a mating bond, but all you're doing is making it sound more appealing." He ran his fingers through my hair, causing my eyes to flutter shut for a moment as I enjoyed the sensation. "Given the choice between a happy eternity with you and the lifetime of loneliness that would wait for me if I ever left Wonderland, I'd choose you every time."

"Even though we've only known each other a short while?" His conviction surprised me. "Doesn't the prospect of living the rest of your life with a man you've just met give you reason for concern?"

He caressed the hair behind my ear, which would have caused my hind leg to thump if I had been in rabbit form still. "Before your magic touched me, absolutely. But what I felt earlier when your powers combined with mine was the single best experience of my life. If mating you meant an eternity of feeling that amazing, we can do it now if you want." He looked into my eyes with no hint of doubt. "If fate says I'm yours, then I must be, right?"

"*Mine*." The word escaped from me as a primal growl before I claimed his lips in a passionate kiss. If I thought the smell of him had driven me wild, it was nothing compared to the taste of him. It unleashed the wildness inside of me as I delved deeper.

Alistair tugged me closer with a whimper of pleasure as he submitted to me. I yearned to go even further, but I owed him the courtesy of showing some restraint.

When I drew back, he looked at me with wonder. "*Wow.*" He brushed some of the hair that had fallen around my face behind my ear. "An eternity of that, please."

I kissed him again, more gently this time. He was mine, so I didn't need to rush. But I couldn't get enough of the way he opened for me and melted against me with a moan. My soul burned for him, making my cock achingly hard as it begged me to make him mine since he had consented. But I wanted to give him some time to process what being a lifelong mate really meant.

He looked at me with confusion when I paused. "Why are you stopping?"

"While I am gratified by your enthusiasm, it's not fair to mate you the same day you found out about it." I caressed his cheek. "I can wait a little longer for you to have time to understand what it means and ask more questions. It's a lifelong commitment and not something you should rush into."

It surprised me to end up on my back with Alistair pinning me to the bed. "That's sweet of you to worry about that, but I have *needs.*" He rocked his hardness against mine. "Why don't you magic off our clothes so we can do something about it?"

I could deny him nothing, so I did as he requested. It made it so much better when he thrust his arousal against my answering one as he leaned down to give me a hungry and demanding kiss. I tugged him closer as I opened for him, enjoying our tongues dueling for dominance.

Even though it was playing with fire, I gave in to the urge to let my magic mesh with his again. We both cried out as the echoing pleasure between us intensified. He rocked against me with urgency and needy noises that drove me wild as I pulled him down for another demanding kiss.

When I took both of our pricks in hand, he only needed a few pumps before he came with a soft cry. The explosion of ecstasy rocketed through our magical connection, pushing me over the edge. My cum mixed with his on my stomach, driving me and my beast wild with lust.

It stunned me when Alistair shifted down, allowing him to lick our combined releases off my skin. He grinned up at me when his actions earned him a rumble of approval from my beast. "Does this count as grooming?" He lapped up another taste with a hum of pleasure.

"Is there some reason you're trying to tempt my beast into mounting you?" I asked with a laugh.

Alistair's eyes were bright with amusement. "Is it working?"

I used my magic to clean us both. "A little too well, actually."

He pouted at being denied. "Hey, I wasn't finished."

I withdrew from his magical connection before my

beast decided it didn't want to wait any longer to form a mating bond with Alistair. "My beast does not share my desire to give you time to grow used to the idea of being our mate. Your erotic display risks pushing it to act before you're ready."

"So, you're saying I shouldn't get on all fours with my ass up to tempt it?" Alistair asked with a wicked grin.

I chuckled, even as my beast went on a wild rampage inside of me at the thought of Alistair in such a tantalizing position. "Please save that for later. I don't think I have enough resistance left to stop my beast from reacting if you did that."

Alistair sighed as he moved to sit beside me. "Well, if I'm not allowed to tempt you or your beast into mating me tonight because you want to be a proper gentleman, would you like me to groom you for real?"

My heart swelled at his desire to embrace a part of my animal heritage. "I'd actually like that very much. It has been a long time since someone has done that for me." Despite my beast's protests at losing our opportunity to claim him tonight, I sat up and turned my back to Alistair.

"Twinkle, may I please have a brush?" One appeared in Alistair's hand. "Thank you! Is there a right way to do this?"

"The brush is enchanted to painlessly remove knots

without snagging on them, so top to bottom works just as well as going from the bottom up."

"Wow, that must be nice with hair as long and thick as yours." Alistair gathered a section, taking great care as he ran the brush through my hair. "I've always had short hair, so this is the first time I've ever combed such long hair."

"You're doing a lovely job of it." It pleased me on a soul-deep level, making my beast rumble with contentment at being tended to with such great care.

"Wait, are you *purring*?" Alistair asked in amazement.

I closed my eyes as I savored being groomed. "Mmhmm."

"Huh, I thought only cats purred." Alistair sounded amazed.

"Have you never been around rabbits before?"

He shook his head. "Not long enough to know they purred. That's so adorable." He made a sympathetic noise. "Poor Cheshire, though. Cats also show their love by grooming, so he would really purr if King Rei did this for him, wouldn't he?"

"When Rei was still a prince, he would spend hours combing Cheshire's hair while they talked. In truth, I had always been a little jealous of that back then since I had never had a mate do that for me." My heart hurt for my oldest friend. "Cheshire misses it, although he never speaks of it."

Alistair sighed. "I know it's not my place, but how can King Rei not see how much he's hurting Cheshire?"

"And himself," I added. "I have tried everything within my power to make him understand that being happy with Cheshire would be the best thing for the kingdom. But as you've seen, he is a particular breed of stubborn that does not give in easily to inconvenient things like logic."

"Did people have a problem with him being together with Cheshire when he was a prince?"

I chuckled at the memories. "Oh, it outraged the court, owing to Cheshire's penchant for playing tricks on those who disapproved of him. But it humored Rei back then, when it didn't matter in his eyes because he was the third prince. It's different when he's king. In his own weird way, he thinks he's protecting Cheshire from the people's disapproval."

"Maybe I'm wrong, but it seems like Cheshire doesn't care what people think of him, right?"

I smiled at his observation. "You are quite correct."

"And who could hate Cheshire? He's so charming!" Alistair tutted as he continued running the brush through my hair. "So, what is King Rei really afraid of?"

"As close as we are, I honestly don't know the answer to that." I sighed with many long years of frustration. "It's almost like he's afraid that if he's with Cheshire, the people will rise up to take Cheshire away from him. To him, it's safer to not be with Cheshire at all."

Alistair made a frustrated noise. "But not being with Cheshire *also* means he could lose him. How does he not see that?"

It was hard sitting on the sidelines and watching someone I cared for so much be so unkind to himself. "He feels damned, no matter what he does."

"Then, wouldn't it be better to be damned and happy than to be damned and miserable?" Alistair's huff of frustration was adorable.

"One would think. My only hope at this point is that Prince Renner comes to the kingdom, which will force King Rei to *finally* act."

Alistair separated another section of my hair to comb with loving attention that I was soaking up. "How?"

"Because he will have an inescapable reason to make a choice between being with the man he truly loves and being with somebody he could never love for the sake of his kingdom. As much as he will struggle with that decision, in his heart of hearts, I know King Rei can't bear the thought of being with anyone who isn't Cheshire."

Alistair was quiet for a long moment. "Do you think he'll choose Cheshire over his royal duty to be with Prince Renner?"

"A mate can only love their fated mate. That is why

King Rei is so unhappy, because he's denying himself the one thing he *needs* to survive and be happy." It was painful to watch as a friend. "The only thing that can stop an engagement to Prince Renner from happening is if King Rei forges a mating bond with Cheshire, which will make him ineligible for marriage to anyone else. He will have no choice but to go public with their relationship under those circumstances."

"Wait, I'm confused. They don't have a mating bond already?"

"Yes, there is the pesky detail that Cheshire never *told* King Rei that they're fated mates. He's just as stubborn about wanting King Rei to choose him before he knows about being fated mates."

Alistair continued brushing my hair as he pondered over the confusing situation. "But wouldn't telling King Rei about their connection help him come to terms with his relationship with Cheshire?"

I made an uncertain noise. "King Rei is not a fan of fate, since he believes that forced him into his current royal role. I understand Cheshire's reservations about telling him. But Cheshire will eventually have to explain everything in order to mate. Prince Renner will give them no choice."

"Isn't that unfair to Prince Renner, though?"

It was sweet that Alistair was concerned for somebody he had never met before. "A bit. But he's only just coming of age, so he is still young and has plenty of time to find a partner who will love him the way he deserves. King Rei will never be that person for him, although by all accounts, Prince Renner is a generous and kind man who would make a wonderful consort for a king."

"You don't think Cheshire will do anything to the prince if he comes here, do you?"

It was a fair question. "Oh, I can almost guarantee that he will be up to his old tricks—and quite a few new ones. But from the research I've conducted on Prince Renner, I've discovered he is a rare fan of Cheshire's and is fascinated by shifters and magic. I don't think Cheshire's pranks are going to work how he intends because of that."

The revelation made Alistair stop mid-brush. "You've done surveillance on Prince Renner already?"

"I knew he was coming of age soon, so I sent scouts to do some digging to be prepared well ahead of time for any prospects. It's what makes me confident that Prince Renner is such a good person King Rei will feel obligated to tell him the truth of who his heart belongs to."

It surprised me when Alistair hugged me from behind, resting his chin on my shoulder. "You're so amazing. That's great that you care enough about King Rei and Cheshire to do that."

"I'll do anything for those I love."

He shifted to sit in front of me. "Including me?"

"And most especially including you." I leaned

forward and captured his lips in a sweet kiss. Now that I had found my mate, I would never run away from him the way King Rei did from Cheshire. It was inconceivable to me. I thanked all my lucky stars that my mate was quite happy to have me by his side. I couldn't wait to claim him as mine forever.

FIFTEEN
ALISTAIR

Bianco took over the responsibility of grooming me by combing my hair next. It seemed silly when I didn't have long, luscious locks like him, but he appeared quite content to tend to me. I enjoyed the experience bringing us closer together.

It raised an interesting question, though. "Is it normal for shifters to not want their mates?"

"Normally, a mate is the best thing that can ever happen to you. In the past, their refusal to accept their mates would have been very strange. But now, it's so uncommon to have a mate, who knows what normal is anymore?" Bianco chuckled to himself. "In a place known for being mad, being normal is quite an abnormal thing, indeed."

"What do you mean it's uncommon to have a mate now?"

"The ability to shift and forge our mating bonds requires access to magic. But when Alice took the magic out of Wonderland, there was none left for those who weren't touched by her." Bianco tutted. "It meant that whatever form a shifter was in when she left was the form they've been stuck in ever since. They don't have enough magic to shift into another form, nor do they have enough to forge a mating bond."

"So, if you hadn't been around Alice and had been in rabbit form when she left, you'd permanently be a rabbit?" It sounded like an awful fate to me for someone who was used to being a person.

He nodded. "Precisely. It's only because of our closeness that I have access to the magic that gives me the ability to shift between my forms and forge a mating bond with you in the future. However, while I'm fortunate to have my powers, they haven't been full strength since she left."

It fascinated me but also gave me a realization. "But if King Rei doesn't have any magic, how could he form a mating bond with Cheshire?"

"Humans in Wonderland have always had a low level of latent magic that they cannot manifest, but a shifter mate could tap into that to finish the mating bond. It is very faint in King Rei, but a glimmer of it is there."

Every revelation gave me a new question. "When

you free magic from within me, would he gain the ability to use magical powers?"

Bianco made an uncertain noise. "There is always a chance of it, but I would say it is unlikely that normal humans could command it the same way shifters can. You, of course, would most likely be an exception as a descendant of Alice. But all the shifters who have been stuck in a single form will be able to shift freely, forge mating bonds, and use magic again."

I turned to face him. "Are you sure you don't want to make that happen tonight?"

He placed a gentle kiss on my forehead that caused my heart to flutter. "While your eagerness pleases me, we should wait a little longer for you to grow used to the idea. I don't want you rushing into something and spend a lifetime regretting it."

"I'd never regret it." While it was a new concept to me, I could feel the rightness down to my bones. "I have some questions that will make me blush, though."

He guided me to lie on the bed, then surprised me when he sprawled on top of me. "Ask away."

I wrapped my arms around him, finding the weight of him reassuring. "While I'm not overly familiar with shifter books, I know they tend to feature wolves and dragons, which are creatures that have a very strong alpha culture with who is dominant in the relationships. But how does that work in rabbits?"

"We certainly have a hierarchy with each other, but

as a human, you fall outside of that boundary." Bianco toyed with the hair at the base of my neck, making me smile. "In general, I suppose it would be fair to say that I'm too submissive in a dominant role and too dominant in a submissive role to be much of anything other than me."

I had to laugh. "Sorry, you lost me. Can you spell that out for me?"

"An alpha cannot submit. An omega can *only* submit. The binary implies you must be one or the other. But I can be a dominant force as the court mage or submissive in my position as it relates to serving the king. At the same time, I regularly defy his authority to try talking some sense into him, which is not something an obedient omega would ever do. Perhaps it would be different if King Rei was a rabbit." Bianco made an amused sound. "That is a very long way to say I am an alpha, omega, and neither at the same time. We are equals in a partnership, if that is your concern."

I couldn't resist stroking his soft hair. "It's not a concern, per se. I just want to make sure that I'm not breaking some unwritten rabbit rule by doing or saying something that will ruin the mood later."

"Ah, I see. You're referring to specific mating practices."

I blushed at him stating it so matter-of-factly. "Yeah."

"A mating ritual is about forming an unbreakable

union between two equal mates," Bianco said. "It's about setting aside that binary to demonstrate your love. It requires a complete circuit between the partners to honor that partnership."

I tried not to get frustrated by my lack of comprehension. "Sorry, you've lost me again. How does that work?"

"To be technical about it, you will come inside of me, allowing the first part of the bond to take hold. I will then come inside of you next while gently biting at your neck to complete the bond between us and end the ritual that shows we are equals in our relationship."

The thought of being intimate without barriers was enough to bring more heat to my cheeks, even as it stirred my arousal. "That's really fascinating. I assumed it would have required only me submitting to you with my ass up in the air."

"That wouldn't be much of an equal partnership." Bianco propped himself up to look down at me. "I'm not interested in dominating or being submissive. I'm looking forward to the pleasure of being together. Position is irrelevant as long as we're enjoying each other. Although, having said that, my beast will almost certainly insist on being the one to mount you from behind to complete the mating bond."

I guided him down for a kiss. "I'm fine with that. It sounds hot as fuck to get railed by your beast."

Bianco arched an eyebrow. "For a human who

comes from a world without shifters, you seem remarkably fine with the idea of my beast sexually dominating you."

"What can I say? It's kinky, and I'm super into it." It was difficult not to laugh at the surprised expression my words earned me. "Do we have to wait? Because I don't need to be a virgin for one more day when I don't have to."

Bianco gave me another kiss that I savored. "As tempting as that is, it has been a long day. It would be better for you to rest."

It was hard not to pout. "Does that mean you're leaving?"

"You say that like you wish for me to stay," he said with a smile.

"That's because I do."

"How could I ever tell you no?" Bianco got up to pull the covers over me. In the blink of an eye, he changed his outfit into a beautiful pair of mauve silk pajamas that brought out the color of his eyes. He then slid into bed next to me, wrapping me up in his embrace.

I relaxed into his hold as Twinkle turned off the lights. Being held by Bianco was amazing. I was more than ready to sign up for a lifetime of cuddles with him. "Good night."

He kissed my bare shoulder. "Sleep well, my sweet Alistair."

While I wanted to stay up and memorize every detail about the perfect moment, after such an eventful day, I drifted off into dreams.

Waking up alone in bed the next morning was a major disappointment. It was enough to make me wonder if everything that happened with Bianco was a dream. But the hairbrush on the nightstand gave me the confidence that my wonderful evening hadn't been a figment of my imagination.

Sensual memories of Bianco's passionate kisses made my cock harden. The thought of him mating me got me all hot and bothered, especially when I pictured his beast taking me hard from behind. Once again, I faced the dilemma of pleasuring myself while being watched by a magical entity and at risk of Cheshire deciding it would be a great time to visit.

But my need was too strong to resist. At least the covers would hide what I was doing from any sudden prying eyes that might appear.

I took my arousal in hand, moaning as I worked it while thinking of Bianco taking things further the previous night.

"You're so beautiful," Bianco murmured, his hand

sliding down from my heart to wrap around my hard length and start working it. "And you're mine."

"All yours." I arched up under his confident grip, aching for more. "Please, I need more."

"You know I would deny you nothing." *He moved down, allowing him to rim my entrance with his fingers.* "Is this what you want?"

What I *really* wanted was Bianco to be with me for real instead of only pleasuring me in a fantasy while I jerked off under the sheets.

That was why it came as a surprise to hear Bianco greet me in an amused tone. "Good morning, sunshine."

I cried out in shock at the sight of him standing next to the bed so suddenly. Grabbing a pillow from behind me, I used it to hide my lap as I sat up to face him. "What are you doing here?" And seriously, was there some unwritten rule in Wonderland that I wasn't allowed to masturbate without interruption? Because that shit was getting *really* old.

"Well, I *was* on my way to meet with my assistant before breakfast, but you seem to have summoned me here." Amusement danced in his beautiful pink eyes. "I suspect the reason why is what you're trying to hide with that pillow."

Maybe it was all the blood rushing south, but his words weren't making sense to me. "How did I summon you here? I don't even know how to do that."

Bianco reached over to drag the pillow away. "Did

you perhaps think, 'I wish Bianco was here,' while plea-suring yourself?"

My face burned from getting caught red-handed. "How would that summon you?"

"Remember the white rabbit ring on your finger?" Bianco peeled back the duvet cover, but I clung to the sheet underneath for the sake of preserving my modesty. "As you will recall, I explained it has the power to bring me to your side whenever you want or need me."

"But I didn't mean to!" It embarrassed me I had prevented him from going to his meeting for such a selfish reason.

"Would you prefer me to leave?" He tugged the sheet out of my grip, revealing my humiliating situa-tion. Rather than gloating, he knelt on the bed and crawled over my body in a sensual display that made my dick twitch with need. "Or do you want me to take care of you?"

I needed to know one thing before agreeing. "Are you going to get in trouble for being late for your meeting?"

"You're so cute for worrying," he said in a fond voice that turned my insides to lava. "I'm sure Twinkle would send a note to my assistant telling him it's canceled. You and your needs are *much* more important."

Before I could protest, Bianco sealed my mouth with his. I moaned into the kiss as his hands traveled over my body, stoking the lust within me to a roaring blaze. By the time he reached my cock, I trembled from how badly I needed him to touch me. I couldn't stop the breathy pleading noises for more as I grew tense the lower he moved.

"Do you want me to pleasure you with my mouth?" Bianco asked in a sensual rumble that made me quake with need.

"Yes, anything, *please!*" To say I was desperate was a massive understatement.

My breathing hitched when Bianco let me slide into the wet warmth of his mouth. He bobbed his head along my length while swallowing, sending me soaring on a lusty high.

I couldn't stop the noises escaping from me. I reached down and entangled my fingers in his soft hair, getting off on the silken strands sliding against my skin while he moved. His tongue was doing magical things as I panted and pled for more.

He took me so deep that I had to wonder if he had any kind of gag reflex at all. Him swallowing around me made my toes curl as I rocked against him with needy noises. My satisfaction spiraled to dizzying new highs that left me breathless.

When Bianco hummed low in his throat, I came while gasping his name. He licked me clean with an approving murmur. "The taste of your ecstasy is intoxicating. But as much as I would love to continue, I have a breakfast meeting with King Rei and a diplomat from Mirrorland that I can't afford to miss."

"But what about you?" I reached down to cup his hardness through his pants. "Can I please take care of you before you go?"

Bianco rocked into my hand with a groan. "I would love nothing more, but it will have to wait until later."

"Oh, I see how it is. You're afraid I'll suck at giving a blow job, aren't you?"

"I believe sucking is the very point of it," he said in a teasing tone. "As delightful as the prospect of having your mouth on me is, I cannot miss such an important meeting between the king and a diplomat." He gave me a tender kiss goodbye I savored. "I promise I'll make it up to you later tonight."

"Shouldn't *I* be the one making it up to *you*?" I pointed out with a pout. "It's not fair I got all the pleasure, and you get an unsatisfied hard-on in return."

"I'll be fine, my love. Since I'll be gone so long, you should go for a walk in the palace gardens. It's a beautiful day." With another kiss, he hurried away to his next meeting.

I stretched out on the bed with a sigh, equal parts satisfied and guilty that Bianco hadn't allowed me to take care of him after he gave me such toe-curling pleasure. But the experience left me more convinced than before that he was my mate—and it wasn't just because he gave the best blow jobs *ever*.

Since I had nothing else to do after eating breakfast, I took Bianco's advice. Of course, I got hopelessly lost before a kind servant brought me to the royal gardens.

As I wandered around the beautiful greenery and impressive fountains, a large butterfly with rainbow wings flew toward me.

"Vivalter? Is that you?" I asked. I hoped it was, otherwise, I'd feel absurd.

The butterfly shifted into the most confusing person I had met in Wonderland so far. Vivalter wore lavender robes trimmed with a blue ombre pattern, which fluttered in the gentle breeze. Like yesterday, his rainbow wings remained in his human form, giving him the appearance of an ethereal fae. "Hello, Alistair," he greeted me in his mellifluous tenor voice. "You seem lost yet again."

"Do you mean metaphorically or locationally?" It seemed like an important difference with someone like him.

He studied me with his indigo eyes that seemed to see straight through me before humming with interest. "Lost and yet you've found your way. Interesting." He began walking, so I fell into step beside him. "I should congratulate you. It seems you have made good progress with Bianco."

I flushed at the implication. Was it because he could smell Bianco on me since I hadn't bathed, or was it something he had seen in visions? "It's been wonderful getting to know him." When Vivalter didn't comment, I pushed to get some information. "We don't have fated mates where I come from, so that was a bit of a surprise."

"A pleasant or unpleasant one?"

The question surprised me. "A very pleasant one, actually." It wasn't my place, but I burned with curiosity. "It fascinates me that every shifter has a perfect mate."

"For something so perfect, it often takes a great deal of searching to find that which is yours. And those like poor March are destined for a long wait, which is far from perfect."

I told myself to stay out of it, but I couldn't. "What about you? Do you know who your mate is?"

"Can you ever really know anything?" Vivalter asked in an airy voice, clearly avoiding the subject.

"I mean, according to Bianco, you know by the smell of someone that they're your mate. Plus, you're a seer, so I would think it would be easier for you to know who that person was than most, right?"

Vivalter paused in front of a large fountain, which had an impressive griffin sculpture as the centerpiece. He was silent as he studied it.

Since I had already committed myself to an awkward conversation, I forged ahead. "Because you were so close, I thought you and Hatter were mates, actually."

"Are you aware of the butterfly's burden?" Vivalter's sudden change in topics confused me.

"What's that?"

"By evolving from a lowly caterpillar to a beautiful butterfly, we become the harbingers of change for the entire world." Vivalter began walking again, so I hurried to catch up.

I didn't quite see what he was getting at. "Because butterflies are creatures of change?"

"Precisely." He was silent as we continued meandering. "The butterfly's burden means that every action we take, everything we decide not to do, it all has consequences for changing the world. One wrong flap of our wings, and we can cause calamity in a neighboring kingdom."

"Oh, we call that the butterfly effect where I'm from." It was a relief that I understood what he was talking about for once. "But it's not a real thing. It's an unproven theory that a butterfly flapping its wings can trigger a tornado somewhere else."

Vivalter sighed. "Far from being a theory, it is the burden every butterfly lives with. As a butterfly shifter gifted with the ability to be a seer, I must be the most careful with my actions. Timing is everything."

"So, you're saying if you mate too soon with Hatter,

it could cause the downfall of the Kingdom of Hearts or something?"

"Or something," Vivalter agreed with a faint smile. "It is fortunate that cats do not share the same problem. My brother's special brand of chaos would create all kinds of havoc."

"And the world would be a better place for it," Cheshire said, startling me when he appeared draped over his older brother's shoulder. "A little chaos never hurt anyone."

"Some of us take our responsibilities very seriously." Vivalter's tone was disapproving, but he still reached up to give his brother a loving scratch behind the ears.

Cheshire sighed. "How many times do I have to tell you? You're a *cat*erpillar, not a butterfly. If you were a true butterfly, I would be a buttercat with wings." Wings of magic appeared on Cheshire's back and flapped in the sunlight, sending purple sparkles cascading around him before disappearing. "And since I am not a buttercat or a catterfly, you are neither."

"If everything you do has consequences, what happens because you had this conversation with me?" I asked.

"The southern provinces of the Kingdom of Hearts will get some much-needed rain to provide a bountiful crop harvest this season," Vivalter said. "Had I not indulged your curiosity, they would have suffered a terrible famine."

That was a level of pressure I couldn't imagine enduring every day. "Well, I'm glad I could help?"

Cheshire jumped from his brother's shoulder to mine. "You are always a help, dear Alistair." He nuzzled my cheek. "Have you helped yourself to Bianco yet?"

I blushed at the question. "Not exactly."

"Tonight would be a fortuitous occasion to forge a mating bond between you two," Vivalter said, surprising me at how direct his comment was. "It would bring many prosperous centuries to King Rei's reign. Waiting until tomorrow would cause decades of civil strife within the kingdom."

I blanched at the implication. "What about the day after that?"

"Hmm, the less said about that, the better." Vivalter's refusal to specify made me worry even more.

"But wait, I'm not a butterfly. Why would when I forge a mating bond have such severe consequences?"

"It is because you are Alice." It was shocking to get a straightforward answer from Vivalter for once. "Your mating bond will unlock the magic of Wonderland for all, so it is indeed an event with far-reaching consequences. Beyond that, you are free to live your life as you choose without fear."

That was at least a little reassuring. "Thanks for telling me."

"See? You don't *always* have to be *so* cryptic," Cheshire chided Vivalter.

Vivalter arched a very judgmental eyebrow at his younger brother. "You say as if you're any different."

"I don't *have* to be so cryptic, but it's marvelous fun to be." Cheshire snickered as his tail swished behind me. "Now, what else can we play with Alistair while Bianco is away with work?"

I wasn't sure what was in store for me, but it was bound to be an exciting adventure with Cheshire and Vivalter.

"Now that we have finalized the trade treaties, there is one other thing we must discuss," said Maram, the Mirrorland diplomat. She was an older, no-nonsense woman in a modest silver dress.

King Rei tried to feign interest, but I could see the leeriness in the shadows of his red eyes. "Oh?"

"There is the matter of Prince Renner's coming of age." She set aside her paperwork to give the ruler her full attention, who stiffened on his throne at the mention of the name.

"It is sure to be a most frabjous occasion," I said in a warm voice since I knew he would want to say as little as possible about the subject.

She gave me a small smile. "King Otto and Queen Emme are excited to be hosting a grand ball to celebrate the momentous day. They are also hoping they will be able to announce their son's engagement to everyone in attendance."

Relief washed over King Rei. "A hearty congratulations to Prince Renner for finding a suitable partner so soon. Truly, an event worthy of such felicitous festivities."

She hid her laugh behind her hand. "It will certainly be a wonderful day once he has chosen his betrothed. But that is indeed what I wished to speak with you about today. It is King Otto and Queen Emme's most fervent wish for you to have a marriage interview with Prince Renner when he visits the Kingdom of Hearts next month."

King Rei's jaw tightened as he nervously glanced around the room for any signs that Cheshire might appear and disrupt the delicate conversation.

When he remained silent, Maram continued. "As the sixth son, Prince Renner is well suited to be a king's consort. He is gentle and kind, with the benefit of a quick wit and delightful sense of humor that could charm even the prickly ambassador from the Kingdom of Spades. He would truly be an asset to your country and would put all those nasty rumors to rest."

King Rei arched an eyebrow as his tone turned defense. "Nasty rumors?"

"There is a great deal of talk about that untrustworthy cat shifter often being spotted near your palace,"

Maram said with strong disapproval. "Those with too much time on their hands whisper it's because Cheshire has cast a spell over you and is your forbidden lover."

It pained my heart to watch King Rei struggling to control his reaction. "People judge what they do not understand." He stiffly drew himself up to his full height. "While it is true that Cheshire lives in my lands, he is not a threat to my kingdom or throne. I have no lover, forbidden or otherwise. It would behoove you not to mention such tawdry gossip as if it were fact, ma'am."

She gave a disdainful sniff. "That as it may be, having Prince Renner as your consort would put an end to all of that gross unpleasantness." She pinned the king under her gaze. "There's no reason for you not to consent to a marriage interview, unless, of course, the rumors are true."

King Rei tightened his hand into a fist as he took a steadying breath. When I started to speak for him, he stopped me. "Fine," he said in a flat voice. "You may arrange a palace visit for Prince Renner to meet with me. Bianco will handle all the details. But I make no promises beyond that."

"Wonderful!" Maram lit up with delight at getting her way. "In that case, I will take my leave and begin arrangements at once. Honorable Bianco, I shall be in touch once I have Prince Renner's schedule. It was a pleasure as always, King Rei." She left with a formal bow, sweeping out of the room with a swish of her dress.

King Rei trembled with barely contained rage. "Damn it!" He hid his face in his hands with a groan. "She played me like a chess piece!"

My heart was full of sympathy for my friend. "You didn't have a choice. For the sake of diplomacy, you had to agree to meet Prince Renner for a marriage interview," I gently reminded him. "The only way out is to formally make Cheshire your consort."

"You heard what she said. People already think he's cast a spell to bewitch me. There will be a revolution if I do that. But he's going to be *so* hurt by this. It's cruel beyond compare, but I don't have a choice! Damn this crown!" King Rei took it off his head and threw it across the room in frustration. "I don't want to do this to him!"

"Rei, as your closest friend, I'm begging you to put an end to this farce," I pleaded, deliberately dropping his royal title. "Facing the consequences once will be far less arduous than torturing yourself daily for years on end."

But King Rei was past the point of listening. "I can't even imagine what payback he will mete out to me and Prince Renner for doing this to him. And the worst part is, I'll deserve it for this betrayal. He'll never forgive me for this. And why should he?"

"Will Cheshire be upset? Absolutely. But he will be upset that they put you in this position, not at you for doing what you must," I reminded King Rei. "He will most likely aim his ire at Prince Renner when he arrives and try to chase him off. More than payback, what you need to be prepared for is Cheshire stepping up his efforts to persuade you to be with him. Because when he grows desperate at the thought of losing you, he won't stop until he makes you his."

King Rei was quiet for several long moments. "I'm so tired of saying no to him. I hate not falling asleep with him in my arms every night, then waking up in my enormous bed alone every morning. I miss being *his* Rei instead of the untouchable King Rei. I miss loving him freely, and he knows it. No matter how much I tell myself I'm not allowed to be with him, my heart is still his. I'm reaching my breaking point, Bianco," King Rei said, his voice cracking with the pent-up emotions over his situation. "I don't know how much longer I can keep resisting him."

"Then choose happiness and end this misery once and for all," I urged him.

Despite his passionate outburst, King Rei fell back on old arguments. "But my people will never allow it. I can't be the selfish ruler who prioritizes his needs over those of my kingdom."

It was difficult not to grow frustrated with his stubbornness. "You're their bloody king! If you tell them to like your consort, they will do so. If you hide him in the shadows, they will continue to distrust him."

"I'm not a dictator," he said with a finality I knew better than to argue against. It was a major point of contention with him because of the former Queen of Hearts and his oldest brother's madness and tyrannical ways. "Until I figure out how to handle this, you can't tell him."

I held in a sigh as I gave a formal bow. "As you wish. But he *will* find out, eventually. I just hope you're prepared for that."

"How are your preparations going with Alistair?" King Rei asked.

The sudden shift in topics was expected, given how uncomfortable he was discussing Cheshire finding out about the marriage interview with Prince Renner. "I believe I will be able to conduct the ceremony to free the magic within him far sooner than expected."

"Really?" He looked up at me with surprise. "Why is that?"

"I received some clarification about the specific wording of Vivalter's prophecy that was very enlightening about what kind of bond Alistair needed to form in order to return the magic to Wonderland." I still felt like the world's biggest dunce for not realizing it sooner. "It was a type that has fallen out of favor since Alice disappeared, so I had almost forgotten about it entirely."

He tilted his head as he regarded me with curiosity. "What is it?"

"A mating bond that only shifters can form with their fated mates."

"I thought that was the stuff of fairy tales?" King Rei rubbed his chin with a thoughtful expression. "Surely, if it was real, Cheshire would have mentioned it to me."

"Perhaps it is you who should mention it to him the next time you meet," I said, unable to stop myself from indulging in a little meddling. He certainly deserved to play an unexpected trump card against Cheshire on the subject. "But I can assure you, fated mates and mating bonds are very real. They used to be common until the magic left Wonderland and put an end to the practice."

"Wait, so does that mean Alistair is a shifter? Since he can form a mating bond with someone?"

I shook my head. "No, but his mate is."

King Rei looked stricken before he regained control of his reaction to compose his face into a neutral expression. "It's not Cheshire...is it?" Despite his best attempts, his upset was visible. "You said that Alistair was fond of that damn cat already, so is that because—is it because they're mates?"

I let an uncomfortable silence drag between us just long enough for King Rei to process how distraught the idea had made him before I put him out of his misery. "No, Alistair is my mate."

King Rei couldn't hide his relief. "Oh! In that case, congratulations are in order. You deserve all the happiness in the world together." It touched me that his words were sincere.

"Thank you." I couldn't resist taking one more chance at helping King Rei make the right decision. "Cheshire has a mate, though. I would encourage you to ask him about it the next time you see him. I believe you would find it a very enlightening and helpful conversation."

A storm passed through King Rei's eyes. "Wait, if he has a mate, why does he spend all his time chasing me?"

"Why, indeed?" I hummed with interest. "I'll leave you to ponder that."

Despite King Rei's protest, I walked out of the meeting with a slight flounce in my step. Maybe it would be my lucky day that I had dropped enough hints that King Rei would *finally* take the initiative when he saw Cheshire again. It was unlikely, but I always liked to dream big.

I headed for Alistair's room once I finished everything I needed to take care of for the day. A curious sound greeted me, so I approached his bedroom with interest.

Alistair was naked on top of the bed, stroking his erection with the slightest arch in his back. Hearing him whimper my name was deeply gratifying. As much as I wanted to join in the fun, I was enjoying the show.

When I crossed my arms and leaned against the doorframe, I drew Alistair's attention. He cried out as he tried to hide his arousal. "Shit! Please tell me I didn't accidentally summon you again."

I chuckled at his reaction. "No, I finished my meeting and came up here to check on you."

"Is there some unwritten rule that I'm not allowed to jerk off in Wonderland? Because this is the third time in a row I've been caught in the middle of trying, and I'm getting *really* frustrated. I *just* want to come!"

"Third time?"

Alistair's cheeks flushed a becoming shade of pink. "Cheshire popped in on me in the bathroom the first time."

While I logically knew I had nothing to fear from the cat shifter, it still displeased my beast to know that Cheshire had witnessed something meant for my eyes only. "I'll have to reprimand him later."

"He obviously wasn't interested. It was more embarrassing than anything else." Alistair sighed with frustration. "Is there a secret way to masturbate so I don't get interrupted?"

"Why do that when I'm here?" I used my magic to make my clothes disappear while I approached him on the bed. "I promise I'll be much more satisfying."

When I positioned myself over Alistair, it surprised

me to have him on top of me as he reversed our positions. "Actually, I believe you said it was my turn first." He kissed me before I could clarify. I gave myself over to his passion, enjoying the way he laid claim to me. The heat from his heavy cock pressing against me drove me wild as he trailed kisses along my jaw and neck, teasing me into a frenzied need as he moved down my body.

By the time he reached my arousal, it was at full mast and begging for attention. "It's finally my turn," he said with glee before he let me slide past his lips and into his wet heat.

I moaned as he put on a show of sucking my dick like it was giving him life. My beast rumbled in approval at the sight of him deriving so much pleasure from taking care of our needs. It clamored within me, begging me to claim our mate.

I tensed when Alistair's fingers slid down to tease my hole. He stopped his oral attention to ask, "What do you use in Wonderland for this part?"

"Normal people would use lube. But I have something better."

His eyes brightened with interest. "Oh, yeah? What's that?"

"Magic." I used it to slick my channel to prepare for what I desperately wanted to come next. "You can enter me whenever you want without hurting me."

"Talk about useful." His fingers slid inside me, making me spread my legs farther apart as I took him deeper. "You said I had to come inside you, and you would come inside of me to form the mating bond. But is there anything else I specifically have to do?"

"Leave the magic part to me." I lifted my hips in encouragement. "All I need is you inside me, if you're sure you want to do this now."

"I've never been more sure of anything in my life." Alistair withdrew his fingers before easing his cock into me, almost as if he feared hurting me. But thanks to my magic, there was no pain at all as my body welcomed him. He leaned forward to kiss me, allowing me to merge his light magic with mine. Each pump of his hips helped strengthen the connection between us. The pleasure he received echoed through me via our tenuous link.

I wrapped my arms and legs around him as I held on, arching up under the sexual satisfaction sparking up my spine with every thrust. Combined with the magic merging our souls together, I transcended into a high I had never known before.

Each time he moaned my name, I could feel the bond tightening between us, taking root deep inside, and growing brighter and hotter as we picked up the pace. I was lost in the glow of intense magic, filled with a power I had never experienced before.

He buried his face against my neck with a whimper as he continued rocking against me with increasing urgency. "Feels so good. Love you so much," he gasped, making the connection between us blaze with heat.

"I love you, too."

As soon as I spoke those words, Alistair pushed in as deep as he could and came while crying out my name. The magic flared as it roared to life, starting the formal bond of his soul to mine. I basked in it before my beast took control to continue with the ceremony.

The magic pulsating between us sent me to dizzying new heights of ecstasy as I took a moment to gather my bearings. I didn't resist as Bianco roughly guided me into position on my hands and knees. It surprised me until I realized his beast was in full control, demanding I assume the submissive stance that would please him most.

I shivered when his magic penetrated my entrance, filling me with slick lube that helped him slide into me with ease. The pain I would have expected to experience without preparation was absent as he set a driving rhythm that made me moan and writhe underneath him. It overjoyed me to *finally* no longer be a virgin in any sense of the word.

Every sharp pump of his hips seemed to strengthen the magical bond between us, allowing his pleasure to echo through our connection. It was impossible not to get lost in the overwhelming sensations bombarding me from all angles. I had never felt so good in my entire life.

I didn't resist when Bianco shifted our angle, pressing his body against mine to bite my neck. It wasn't hard enough to pierce the skin, so it didn't hurt. If anything, it was a major turn-on, having him give in to his rabbit instincts as he rutted against me while holding me in place.

I reached my hand back to entangle in Bianco's hair as he pushed my body to its limits. It was almost more pleasure than I could endure, especially when our magical connection sparked wildfire within me that aroused me even more. I could only whimper his name and hold on tight as he masterfully worked my body.

Without warning, he buried himself to the hilt while he dug his teeth in a little more, then came inside me with a deep rumble. A flash of heat exploded between us, making everything turn white as our mating bond fully took hold. The purity of our love dissolved the dark magic within me. As it disappeared, our connection grew more solid, until I felt all of Bianco's emotions. The intensity of it drew my orgasm from me, which triggered another flare of power as it unleashed my light magic to return to Wonderland.

When it was over, I collapsed on the bed, panting as I closed my eyes and basked in the overwhelming euphoria.

Bianco curled up behind me, pulling me into his arms. He nuzzled against me with a contented murmur. *"Our mate."*

It surprised me that he said "our" and not "mine," but I figured it must have been a quirk of his beast.

I replied with the only word I could muster. *"Yours."*

It was the most incredible experience of my life, but unleashing Wonderland's magic had left me too drained. As much as I wanted to stay in the moment, I succumbed to sleep.

When I awoke, it was dark outside while Bianco embraced me from behind. He must have cleaned me up with magic because I didn't have any of the gross stickiness inside of me I would have expected after falling asleep before I could take a bath.

The mating bond thrummed between us with contentment and love. It was a beautiful sensation that made me feel like I had finally come home after being lost for far too long. For the first time, I was whole and at ease, with none of the shadows of anxiety that had always plagued me.

It took an effort to roll onto my back to look up at Bianco. To my surprise, his pink eyes seemed to glow with an unnatural light. It was too fascinating to scare me, especially when the possessive love echoed in our bond.

He caressed my cheek as he gazed down at me with affection. "Our beautiful mate."

"You're Bianco's beast?" I asked. While I had heard him refer to it before, I hadn't realized it was an actual presence I could interact with.

"Yes." He brought my hand up to his lips to kiss my ring finger, then nuzzle against it. "We live to love and protect you. This mark proves it."

Maybe it was because I was still woozy from the magical expenditure earlier, but his words made me *swoon*. "Wait, what mark?"

Twinkle provided a low level of lighting, allowing me to notice a tattoo on my left ring finger of an ornate blue line interwoven with pink. I rubbed it with my thumb in confusion. "You did this?"

"It is proof of our mating bond." He held his hand up to allow me to see his mirroring one. "It is our oath that we will always take care of your every need and desire." Bianco's beast leaned in to give me a passionate kiss, flooding me with his lust. Despite my exhaustion, my body responded as he used magic to slick me inside once again.

Without warning, something changed in the bond. The intense possessiveness faded as loving adoration took over. When Bianco pulled back, his eyes had returned to normal. He gave me a sheepish grin. "Sorry. Please forgive my beast for being a little overeager. I know you need to rest."

"It's fine. He's quite charming." There were worse things in the world than being desired by a very affectionate mate. "Where do you go when he's in control?"

"I'm behind him but still able to experience everything through him since we are one and the same." Bianco shrugged. "It's a little hard to explain."

"So, you were there but not in control during the mating?" I asked.

"I was in control for the first part, when you were inside me, but my beast had to complete the mating bond while claiming you." Bianco caressed my skin, sending shivers through me. "I still felt everything, though. It was the best moment of my life so far."

It seemed terribly unfair to me that Bianco had been forced to take a back seat. "But I want to be with you, too."

"There's plenty of time for that later. You should rest now."

"*Please.*" His beast had gotten me stirred up earlier. I needed more, despite being pleasantly worn out. "I need *you*, Bianco."

He hesitated. "Do you know how difficult it is to tell you no when I can feel how much you want me?"

"Then don't tell me no." I help guided him into position over me. "I promise I can handle it."

It was odd sensing him cave through our new bond. He lifted my hips before he pushed into me, filling me with his hard length. I moaned as he set an easy rhythm, wrapping my legs around his waist as he made gentle love to my body that was enhanced by our magical mating bond.

Getting railed by his beast had been amazing, but I loved Bianco's tenderness as he took his time pleasuring me while caressing me all over. I arched under him with a breathy plea for more. He rewarded me with using a little more force with each thrust, making me cry out as I buried my fingers in his long hair and held on for dear life.

"My mate," Bianco murmured, leaning down to kiss me while he continued rocking my body and sending my pleasure soaring. "My love."

When he reached between us to stroke my arousal, it was too much to bear. I came with a gasp, triggering his release. Feeling him coming inside me was enough to make me experience a second phantom orgasm ripple through me. I whimpered when he leaned down to give me a tender kiss while he embraced me through our bond. It was the best sensation in the world.

I pouted when Bianco used his magic to clean me up as he settled beside me again. "You didn't have to do that right away." I blushed as I admitted, "I enjoy being marked as yours."

It fascinated me to see his eyes flash with the unnatural glow that signaled his beast trying to come to the surface. "I'll keep it in mind in the future." He slung an arm over my chest as he cuddled beside me. "For now, you should rest."

"What about the light and dark magic? It felt like it was released earlier, but I could be confusing it with our mating bond forming—which was incredible, by the way."

Bianco chuckled as he brushed his thumb against my skin. Before he could reply, Cheshire appeared with his trademark grin. "Allow me to answer that." He made himself right at home by curling up on my chest against the crook of Bianco's arm. "The light magic has once again returned to Wonderland. It's the most wondrous thing. The card guards are back, the magical flowers are blooming and singing once more, shifters have their powers back, and I'm more powerful than ever. You've outdone yourself, dear Alistair."

Despite being embarrassed about getting interrupted in an intimate embrace with my new mate, I couldn't resist giving Cheshire some loving pets. "And what about the dark magic?" I thought I had experienced it dissolving, but confirmation would be nice.

"Your love has purified it through your mating bond." Cheshire nuzzled against my hand. "My sincerest congratulations on your union. Your mating mark is quite beautiful, too. It makes you smell even more delightful." It startled me when Bianco growled in response. Cheshire batted him on the nose. "Now, now. There's no need for growls and snarls, most honorable Bianco. Surely, your beast must know I'm not a threat to you or your mate. I am merely stating a fact."

It was an interesting sensation to sense indignation ripple through my mating bond before a hint of contrition appeared.

"My apologies," Bianco said. "My beast is being overly protective of our new mate and hasn't reached a point of being rational yet."

"You are both forgiven." Cheshire curled his tail around himself as he purred. "Besides, it's not as if I am any different with Rei. Mine goes quite mad over my unruly mate."

I understood the sympathetic twinge coming through the bond from Bianco, but the hint of guilt confused me. It was going to take some getting used to having permanent insights into his emotions.

"Speaking of King Rei, have you visited him today?"

"No, I figured you would be more appreciative of my presence when I offered a report on the status of magic returning to Wonderland. After all, you're currently indisposed after your successful mating." Cheshire's tail flicked rhythmically. "Perhaps if I am feeling benevolent, I shall visit the king tonight while he takes a bath."

"In light of my bonding with Alistair, it would be a great time to tell him about being your mate." Bianco stroked Cheshire's scruff, earning loud purrs for his efforts. "The longer you wait, the less receptive he will be."

Cheshire stood up and did a big stretch, patting his front paws on my chest as he lifted his rear up. "I shall leave you two love bunnies alone to enjoy your newly formed mating bond. Congratulations, my dear friends." With that, he disappeared.

Joy bubbled up within me. "We really did it! We returned the magic to Wonderland!"

"It's been so long since I had full command of my powers I forgot how good it feels to be made whole once more." Bianco summoned swirling pink magic to his hand that sparkled in an impressive display before it faded away. "Wonderland being returned to its former glory is truly something amazing."

"Can I ask you something unrelated to that?"

"Of course," Bianco said with a kind smile. "You're always allowed to ask me anything."

Despite the permission, I hesitated for a moment. "Why did you feel guilty earlier when we were talking to Cheshire about King Rei?"

Bianco sighed as he rested his head on my shoulder. "The diplomat we met from Mirrorland this morning forced King Rei to invite Prince Renner here for a marriage interview. I'm confident it will be the push he needs to choose Cheshire, but it will still sting when he finds out later."

I wrapped my arms around Bianco to hug him. "For

both of their sakes, I hope King Rei makes the right decision."

"He has to," Bianco said with quiet conviction. "But that is a problem for another day. We should rest now."

"Do you mean rest up before the next round or actually sleep?"

He chuckled at my question. "Which do you think?"

"I know which one I'm hoping for." Although I didn't want to move, I stole a kiss to persuade him. I could feel his arousal through our connection. Having a mate was *awesome*. I couldn't wait to find out what other benefits I would have from our mating bond.

EIGHTEEN

BIANCO

The last thing I wanted to do was leave my tempting mate, but my royal duties called. I slipped out while Alistair slept in, hurrying to meet with King Rei in his chambers.

When I arrived, Vivalter was already there and sipping tea. "Congratulations are in order for such a frabjous occasion." He lifted his teacup to me in a toast. "You've done well, my friend."

"I can't believe the magic has returned to Wonderland," King Rei said in awe, gesturing for me to join them at the table. "I don't know how you did it, but we owe you a great deal for doing what many thought was impossible."

"It was my honor." I bowed my head in acknowledgment as I sat down.

"And your great pleasure," Vivalter added with a perverse smirk that brought color to my cheeks.

I rubbed the magical ring on my finger that symbolized my magic unifying with Alistair's. "Yes, it was that as well." Not wanting to get into the private details, I redirected the subject. "What news do you bring, Vivalter?"

He set his teacup down to give us his full attention. "The dark magic has been eradicated, allowing the light to spread freely throughout all the kingdoms of Wonderland. Bianco's actions will bring you many centuries of a prosperous reign, Your Majesty."

While most rulers would have been delighted at the news, King Rei's jaw tightened with displeasure. "Is that so?"

"With your consort at your side, you will have great joy in your life and very few sorrows." Vivalter sipped his tea as he looked King Rei in the eyes. "Prince Renner's upcoming visit next month will indeed bring you much delight."

King Rei's right eyebrow arched upward. "How will it bring me anything but pain and aggravation?"

"Because love is more powerful than that."

"Are you saying I'm going to fall in love with Prince Renner?" King Rei looked aghast at the prospect.

Vivalter dragged out the moment with a long sip of his drink. "He will bring you many gifts. Love is merely one of them."

My heart broke at how upset King Rei became at the news. "Surely, you must be mistaken! I could never love him."

"And yet you will."

The words struck King Rei like a physical blow. He staggered back in his seat. "That's impossible! If I can't be with the person I truly love, then I will be with no one at all."

A heavy silence descended. I took the opportunity to reflect on Vivalter's words. He was rarely so direct. Was it possible that Prince Renner's gift of love would come in the form of helping King Rei choose Cheshire? What if King Rei loved Prince Renner for helping make it possible for him to be with his beloved Cheshire?

"And what of your brother?" King Rei demanded, a slight tremble in his voice.

"Prince Renner has several surprises in store for Cheshire," Vivalter predicted. "Nothing will go as planned, and yet it will all work out in the end."

King Rei rubbed his forehead as he tried to parse through Vivalter's words. "I don't suppose you can be more specific than that?"

"There will be unexpected consequences that are far-reaching for both kingdoms." Vivalter drank his tea. "It shall be fascinating to watch unfold."

King Rei narrowed his eyes. "Might I remind you it is my life and kingdom on the line? Perhaps you should not take such joy in the possibility of a calamity befalling us all."

"There is no calamity to fear, Your Majesty. These changes will be for the best, I assure you."

"You say that, but I don't feel very reassured," King Rei said with a frown. "It sounds like my life is about to become hell when your brother finds out that I've betrayed him by agreeing to allow Prince Renner to come here for a marriage interview. I refuse to believe I will fall in love with him. It's unfathomable!"

"Vivalter didn't say that you would fall in love with Prince Renner, though," I pointed out. "What if his arrival allows you to finally choose the love you have with Cheshire? Surely, that would be a magnificent gift of love that the prince could give you."

"Is Bianco right?" King Rei demanded.

Vivalter shrugged. "Doing what we should is not doing what we must. It is up to you to decide what that means." He stood up with a formal bow. "Please excuse me."

"Thank you for your insights, Vivalter," King Rei said formally. He waited until the butterfly shifter had left to mutter, "Sometimes, I think not knowing is easier than trying to decipher his senseless riddles. No good can come from Cheshire being surprised."

"If you wished to be surprised, here I am," Cheshire said, appearing in King Rei's lap in his human form without warning. He nuzzled against his mate's cheek in greeting.

King Rei wrapped his arms around Cheshire to hold him tight, even as he said, "You shouldn't be here."

"You're right, we should be in bed together instead." In the blink of an eye, they both disappeared, presumably to King Rei's private chambers. Cheshire had certainly been making the most out of having his full powers again.

I said a silent prayer that Vivalter's prophecies had shaken King Rei enough to choose Cheshire once and for all. In the meantime, I had a mate to attend to.

When I returned to Alistair's bedroom, he was naked and about to get dressed. Our bond hummed with immediate arousal, causing me to raise my eyebrows in surprise. "The mere sight of me is enough to arouse you that much?"

"Hell yeah it is." He crooked his finger and gestured for me to move closer. "Why don't you undress so I can ride you in the naughty way?"

It was an invitation I would never refuse. I used my magic to get rid of my clothes before I stretched out on the bed and welcomed Alistair into my arms. He gave me an aggressive kiss that made me rumble with contentment as I indulged him. While my beast preferred to be the dominant one, I quite enjoyed Alistair taking the lead.

"Get me ready so I can ride you hard," he said in between kisses.

I delighted in using my magic to prepare him, getting him slick and stretched as we continued kissing.

"Seriously, that feels so good. I bet you could make me come with just your magic," he said. "We should try it sometime. But right now, I need this."

Alistair gave my prick a few strokes before he lowered himself onto it with a groan of relief. True to his word, he started a fast rhythm as he braced himself on my stomach.

The roughness of it appealed to the primal part of me as I thrust up hard to meet him on his downward bounces. He was beautiful as he arched up with a soft cry, his body rocking ceaselessly in search of ecstasy. It would never cease to amaze me that such a wonderful person was mine for the rest of time.

I reached out to stroke his arousal, causing him to cry out and lose his rhythm. But he quickly recovered, moving with increasing urgency. "Fuck, I *love* having sex," he moaned, making me laugh. "It was worth waiting so long to land the hottest guy in two worlds, whose dick is a magic wand. *Fucking yes*! Bianco!"

Alistair came all over my fist with a shudder, lighting up my insides through our bond with his intense ecstasy that triggered my orgasm. The sexual nirvana I derived from being with my mate had indeed been worth the long wait. I held him when he collapsed on top of me with a satisfied groan, nuzzling against him as my beast purred in contentment from taking such good care of our mate.

"How is it I feel both amazing and like I need more?" Alistair asked, causing me to laugh.

"If you want more, I can certainly give you that." I used my magic to penetrate him, rubbing the spot inside him that could make him come undone.

He cried out as he jerked in surprise. "*Oh!*"

I manipulated my magic to grow within him, earning me the most delightful whimper.

He moved off me to roll onto his back, arching up with another cry as I stroked him with the magic, filling him with my power and making it move faster. His hips pushed down on the sensation as he rocked into it.

When I thought he was becoming too complacent, I gestured with my hand to allow my pink magic to swirl around his cock and start stroking it back to life.

"Oh, *fuck me!*" Alistair cried out with a gasp as he arched up into the feeling. "Shit, how am I already getting hard?"

"Because you have inherited my faster rabbit refractory period through our mating bond." I gestured at my own returning arousal. "You'll also get the benefit of being able to come again as well."

He made an excited noise. "You're seriously telling me I can have multiple orgasms without having to wait long?"

"Indeed, it is a marvelous thing." I waved my hand to expand the magic inside of him and work his length faster. It had the desired result of making him climax a second time with a full-body shudder.

"Marvelous? Try best thing *ever*." He moaned in satisfaction as I released the magic from him. "You deserve a reward for that."

I arched my eyebrows at his assertion. "And what would you suggest?"

Alistair rolled over onto his side and got up on all fours before he stretched out so that his ass was raised in offering. He even had the audacity to tempt me with a little wiggle.

My beast was on him in an instant, rutting against him hard and fast like the rabbit we were. Not content with just that, it used magic to lengthen and thicken our cock until Alistair was shouting our name in between breathless cries of ecstasy. It spurred my beast to guide our mate up to bite his neck while we pounded into him. At such an intense pace, it didn't take much longer before my beast came with a growl, pinning Alistair down on the bed as it thrust until it was spent. The scent of Alistair's third orgasm pleased my beast immensely, leading it to rub our chin against our mate's shoulder and kiss his neck.

Alistair melted into a satisfied puddle with a protracted moan. "Holy hearts of Hell, that was *incredible*."

I pushed my beast back so I could tend to Alistair. "Did my beast hurt you?"

Alistair stretched before rolling onto his side. "No, he rocked my world. You both do." He guided me closer for a kiss. "I really am the luckiest person in all of Wonderland."

"You were meant to be ours." I lay down and guided Alistair to lie on top of me. He was completely boneless as he sprawled out. "Never doubt how much we love you."

Alistair poked at our magical bond as best he could. "With this connection between us, I never have to doubt anything." He sighed in contentment. "I'm *so* glad you found me, and I'm allowed to love you."

"From now until eternity," I reminded him, nuzzling against his hair. "You will always be mine to love."

"Hell yeah I am," he declared with pride. "You promised me a fun adventure of a lifetime, and you certainly delivered on that."

"Our fun adventure is only beginning."

"And the sexy shenanigans are only just getting started," he added, making us both laugh.

I had lived a long time without my fated mate, but I was so glad I finally had him in my life. A life lived in love was indeed a life worth living.

EPILOGUE

ALISTAIR

THREE WEEKS LATER

Since there was only so much sex we could have in a day, Bianco had enlisted my help as the official Alice Ambassador for the Kingdom of Hearts. I thought he was nuts because I wasn't exactly known for being smooth or tactful, but I had to admit, parts of the position were fun. Getting to travel through the kingdom and see the difference that the returned magic had made for people was amazing. I was even more proud of what Bianco and I had accomplished.

The part I wasn't so fond of was preparing for the impending arrival of Prince Renner in a week. "I feel like I'm betraying Cheshire," I complained to Bianco in our room after a long day of working on event planning.

"I know I don't have a choice, but I really don't want to be involved in this."

Bianco gave me a hug before sitting us down on the couch in front of the fireplace. "There is no betrayal here. Cheshire knows about the visit, so nothing is being hidden from him."

"But how can the king interview a potential suitor when his mate is *right there*?" I asked with a huff. "It's so wrong!"

"There isn't a world where King Rei will choose anyone over Cheshire." Bianco stroked my hair to soothe my fears. "Trust me. This is the push he needs to get over his reservations about having Cheshire as his official consort. I promise that this visit from Prince Renner will be the best thing that could happen to King Rei and Cheshire's relationship."

"Are you sure? Because Vivalter's prophecies made it sound like King Rei was going to fall in love with Prince Renner." I couldn't stand the thought of Cheshire being hurt by the ruler making the wrong choice.

"Remember how Vivalter said you needed to form a bonding love but neglected to include the detail about it being a mating bond with me?" Bianco caressed the back of my neck as he embraced me through our magical connection. "I'm confident this is no different. King Rei's love for Prince Renner won't be romantic. It will surely be for allowing him to freely love Cheshire at long last."

"For both of their sakes, I hope you're right."

"Next week should be *very* interesting." Bianco hummed with interest. "I'm quite certain Cheshire will keep all of us on our toes with his mischief in his quest to persuade King Rei to forge their mating bond. It will be exciting times indeed."

I leaned over to hug Bianco. "Hopefully, the cosmic universe will be as kind to them as it has been to us."

"Yes, we have been fortunate to be so blessed." He gave me a tender kiss that lit me up inside like a fireworks finale.

"Hey, I have a great idea." It was hard not to grin at my genius plan.

He could tell something was amiss based on the amusement echoing through our bond, but he was a good sport. "And what would that be?"

"Do we have time for me to fall down your rabbit hole again?"

He laughed at my ridiculous euphemism for topping him but still swept me up into a princess hold to go make all my dreams come true.

Living a fairy-tale romance sure beat the hell out of a dead-end job. My only regret was that I never got to bake a "Fuck you, I quit cake" to tell my awful coworkers how I *really* felt. But getting to be loved by the sweetest rabbit shifter in all of Wonderland more than made up for it. We still had so many adventures to have, and I looked forward to them all.

Curious to see Bianco teach Alistair how to use his new powers? **Claim your copy of Coming Home today!**

Want to see Cheshire and King Rei find their happily ever after together? **Read Cheshire in Heartsland to enjoy their playful royal romance.**

THANK YOU

Thank you for reading **Alistair in Wonderland**. Reviews are crucial for helping other readers discover new books to enjoy. If you want to share your love for Alistair and Bianco, please leave a review. I'd really appreciate it!

Recommending my work to others is also a huge help. Don't hesitate to give this book a shout-out in your favorite book rec group to spread the word.

NEXT IN SERIES

AVAILABLE NOW

Cheshire is determined to convince King Rei to give them a second chance at happily ever after. But what if the only way to do that is for the cat shifter to team up with his enemy?

If you love sweetheart shifters with fated mates, royal romances, and second chances at true love, **read**

Cheshire in Heartsland today by using the QR code below!

Acknowledgments

Alistair and Bianco's story is one I've wanted to tell for a long time, so I appreciate you taking a chance on it! *Alice in Wonderland* was one of my favorite books as a kid because the thought of living in a world with talking cats was my idea of heaven.

Special thanks goes out to my amazing team of beta readers of Amy Mitchell, Raquel Riley, Lindsay Porter, Tammy Jones, Lisa Klein, Kylie Anderson, Cilla May, Dylan Pope, Jennifer Sharon, Missy Kretschmer, and Ashley Krystalf! I'm so lucky to call such wonderful people my friends.

I'm incredibly appreciative of the kind generosity shown to me by Shelia Kilgore, Tammy Jones, Gabriela, and my other Ko-fi supporters who helped make it possible for me to continue being a full-time author.

I also want to thank everyone who recommends my books in Facebook rec threads. It means everything to me that you share my books with other readers. I'm also filled with endless gratitude to all of my ARC readers for taking the time to leave such thoughtful reviews.

Working with Pam, Sandra, and Natasha is a dream come true.

I can't wait to meet again in **Cheshire in Heartsland**!

ABOUT THE AUTHOR

ariella zoelle

WWW.ARIELLAZOELLE.COM

Ariella Zoelle adores steamy, funny, swoony romances where couples are allowed to just be happy. She writes low angst stories full of heat, humor, and heart. But sometimes she's in the mood for something with a bit more angst and drama. If you are too, check out her A.F. Zoelle books.

Get a bonus chapter by using the QR code below!

Printed in Great Britain
by Amazon

25814384R00132